Just Five Mo

CW00405853

Michael Ross

To Catherine,
With my very best
Wishes.
Michael Ross

This beautiful book cover was lovingly designed and produced
by Magdalena Adic. (www.peopleperhour.com)

ISBN: 9781973119821

Other books by this Author:

Memoirs From The S.B.C. Amazon, 2017

CONTENTS

CHAPTERS

P.T.O.

DEDICATIONS

I dedicate this book to my sons, Aidan, Ben and Oliver.

To my Brother, Kevin, who is my rock.

To the Cheshire police who worked tirelessly to catch the perpetrator of this senseless crime.

To Jenna Timmis, the police family liaison officer, who
was always there 24/7 to help and advise.

To Helen and Edwin Taylor, the boy's childminders, who, with their love care and attention, were incredibly helpful.

To the Boys Godmother, Nanette Swindells, who was so instrumental in keeping so much together in those early days. (R.I.P Nanette)

To Ann Ward, Jacquie's best friend, who has also been our best friend, and who has been a loyal supporter ever since.

To Lynda O'Gormon, Jacquie's cousin, who has always been there to fall back on in times of need.

And to all of you out there, who have lost a loved one, with or without children, who may be thinking:

"What can I do?"

"How do I cope?"

"How do I move on?"

Remember the magic words,

Hope and *Time*.

Not forgetting all those kind and generous people that helped correct, read and shape this book: Peter Hough, Josie Manning, Ellie-Rose & Sylvana Savvas, and finally Grammarly Professional!
Thank you very much.

Prologue

We all live our lives to a routine. Day in, day out, we love, we shout. We have the occasional blip, but generally, we cope, adjust and mostly, we move on.

But sometimes, just sometimes, something unbelievable hits us like a sledgehammer, out of the blue, usually when we least expect it!

And sometimes, just sometimes, we have no warning. Not even a hint. And we always imagine it happening to other people. In a sense, we act as if we are bystanders, observers.

And so it was on that fateful sunny spring-like morning in January 2005. It was 8.30am. Sleepily quiet. I was still snoozing in bed. Our boys, who were four and six, were fast asleep. Jacquie was up already, dressed for a power walk with Rosie, our dog.

Silently, Jacquie crept up to me, leant down, lightly kissed me on the cheek, and whispered: "Love you, see you later". And with that, she was gone.

Those were the last words she ever said to me.

CHAPTER 1

Just Five More Minutes

<u>8.30 am</u>

I didn't even hear the back door close as Jacquie left the house. She was very thoughtful like that, closing the door quietly so she would not wake any of us up. She set off with our soft coated wheaten terrier, Rosie, for a power walk, on one of her numerous routes that circled where we lived.

We had arranged to meet some good friends in Liverpool later at midday. The journey would take us a good hour and a half, and Jacquie was well aware she needed to be back and ready to leave by 10.30am.

I stirred, then got up, washed, dressed and downstairs to finish proving the homemade bread rolls I had prepared, as I did most Sunday mornings. I switched the oven on, ready to bake.

<u>9.00am</u>

By now I had woken the boys up. The rolls were in the oven. (I had twelve minutes). I helped the boys get dressed (Jacquie had already put out what they were wearing for that day). After playing the 'catch me' game for five minutes, with lots of laughter, squealing and shouting, they were more or less dressed. I started to make my way downstairs as I heard the 'beep' of the oven timer. Perfect! I quickly laid the table, sat the boys down (Oliver still had his high chair), and we tucked into our breakfast of cereal and hot rolls.

9.30 am

By now I was clearing up, the boys were watching a video or playing with toys in the living room.

And at the back of my mind, almost as an afterthought, I said to myself "Where's Jacquie?". She should have been back by now? But I wasn't worried at all! She was a very gregarious person, very amicable, and on her power walking routes, she would come across dog walkers, fishermen, park keepers, etc. She would always have a word or two with them.

10 am

By now I have cleared up. Washed up, dried up and tidied up, and sorted the boys out so, they were ready to go, but that little voice came back in my head now, with more urgency, she really should have been back by now.

We had a rule. Always take your mobile, in case of emergencies, and it had to be switched on. (Much later, I realised how useless this piece of advice was in this particular case).

10.30 am

I was now getting a little more anxious. Jacquie was an hour late. We should have been leaving now to visit our friends in Liverpool. I was trying to keep the boys occupied, but my mind was on Jacquie.

Questions were coming into my head thick and fast now. Had she fallen?, Had she injured herself? Had she taken a longer route than usual, or had I just not listened when she had told me the day before? At the same time, I expected her to come through the door at any minute, out of breath, apologising for being so late.

I tried her mobile. It rang and rang and then went to voice-mail. That annoyed me slightly. Come on Jacquie, answer, please!

10.45am

I went to the front of the house. I looked left and right and up and down our little road trying to spot her. But no joy. I phoned her mobile again. Straight to voicemail

11.00am

I'm becoming increasingly more worried and, all sorts of scenarios were flying through my head. But now, I was trying to put a plan together, as to what I should do. What should I do?

Right, I could drop the boys off at their Godmother's who lived close by. Then pick one of Jacquie's routes, and start running along it, to see if I could find her. And possibly telephone the police? The problem was, I was still convinced she would walk through the door as if nothing had happened, and I would feel so embarrassed. I tried her mobile, and again it went to voicemail

11.15am

By now, I had decided what to do. Drop the boys off. Run a route. Tell the police. But when? Again I went to the front of the house.

I remember this moment quite clearly, across the valley, I

heard an ambulance siren (The timeframe shows that it must have been the ambulance that was being called out to Jacquie).

And again I phoned. Voicemail. I needed to find the courage to set into motion all my plans, sooner, rather than later.

11.20am

Once more I tried phoning. Voicemail. I now decided, with added determination, I needed to pick a time to start with my plan.

11.25am

Focussing on a time, sticking to it, and putting so many things into action was an incredibly difficult decision to be made at the time. In fact, one of the most difficult I have ever had to make. I wanted to find a corner to creep into and hide, close my eyes and hope it would all go away. I realised that nobody could help me. I was on my own. I would telephone one last time at 11.30am. If there were no answer, I would put into action everything I had planned. There would be no turning back. So now this was it, for the last time, just five more minutes.

11.30am

This made me anxious. This was it. I tried one last time. Her phone rang twice, yet again, I was expecting it to go straight to voicemail, but it didn't!

This time Jacquie's mobile was answered, and took me completely by surprise! My heart missed a beat. It was a man's voice. A voice I didn't recognise.

CHAPTER 2

A & E

"Who is this?" the voice on the other end of Jacquie's mobile phone said. "No! I said, That's my wife's phone, I want to know who *you* are!". "I'm a police officer". He gave me his full name and which force he was with, and I gave him my name and other details, then he said, "Your wife has had an accident, she was found at the bottom of an embankment next to the Peak Forest canal. The ambulance has attended, and she is being taken to A&E at Stepping Hill hospital."

By now, questions are flooding into my head. But the policeman said, "We have found a dog here at the scene, she has a collar on and called Rosie, does this dog belong to you?".
I told him, yes, and then he wanted to know what to do with her? I asked him if he would drop her off with the boy's Godmother who lived very close.

I was just holding everything together, and frustratingly, the policeman would not give any details on how badly hurt Jacquie was. He just kept advising me to make my way to A&E at Stepping Hill hospital in Stockport.

I jumped into the car, and after dropping the boys off with their Godmother, I made my way to the hospital. I half ran into the A&E department of the hospital. It was very busy. I ran up to the admissions desk, behind which were three or four staff who were rushing around. I caught the eye of one and simply said to her "My wife has had an accident, and has just been rushed in". "What's your name please?" she said. "Michael Ross" I replied. Now, suddenly, all those behind the admissions desk froze! They all looked at me. "Mr Ross?" The nurse said, confirming my name. I said yes.

There was a prolonged silence; then immediately I was ushered to the side of the desk and into a little room behind. It was a small room. Two or three ordinary armchairs, a coffee table, a telephone and a window that looked out onto a little patch of grass.

I was brought some tea and biscuits and told I could use the telephone if I needed to, so I telephoned our friends in Liverpool, the boys Godmother and my Mother and Father.

I played it down a little because as yet, I didn't know what had happened, I didn't have enough facts. Ok. Now I'm not stupid, I knew something serious had happened, and I desperately wanted to know, now!

I made a couple more calls, and then into the room walked a Doctor wearing a white coat. He told me that Jacquie had sustained some injuries to her body, but in particular to her head and that she was unconscious.

But what he said next, was chilling. He told me, that the injuries she had sustained to her head are not conducive to injuries you might have had, simply by rolling or tripping down an embankment.

The injuries to her head were serious, and scans of her head were sent to Hope Hospital, in Salford, and it has been decided she needs urgent surgery on her head, so she is in the process of being transferred to that hospital, which is just under an hour away. I said, "May I see her please?" He said, "Well, please give us a few minutes to clear the area, then I will take you to her, but you need to know she is unconscious and for the sake of her injuries, we are keeping her in that state".

As soon as the Doctor went out, two men came into the room, introduced themselves as detectives, and spread out an OS map of the area where we live. They wanted confirmation that Jacquie had taken Rosie out for a walk. In particular, what routes would she have taken when she went for her power walk, how long the routes would have taken to power walk, and did I know which particular route she would have taken. I'm anxious. A little confused, and my head has filled up with all sorts of questions, and suddenly to be confronted with a spread out OS map, not knowing if it was the right way round or upside down was all very confusing. I could not get my bearings simply by looking at the map and was searching for a name or a familiar piece of landscape. I started turning the map through all points of the compass, desperately trying to spot something familiar. I took a deep breath. Tried calming down, looking more carefully, then slowly I started to recognise some of the routes, some of the names, which I traced with my finger for the Detectives

But she had a number of routes, and once I was able to get my head around the map, I managed to indicate three or four routes she could have taken. Then they suddenly wrapped everything up and left.

In came the Doctor and took me into a large curtained area within the A&E department. I couldn't help but notice lots of plastic bags of blooded tissues and bandages, some around the base of the bed, some spilling out of yellow plastic bags.

I learnt later that she was losing so much blood, she had to have at least one full blood transfusion. What I saw was a shock! Jacquie was wired up to various machines, IVs etc. Her head was completely bandaged (I remember seeing some of her blonde hair coming out from underneath the head bandage from around her neck area).

Her hands were bandaged, especially her left one. She had been put in one of those surgical all in ones with a split up the back.

She had little cuts on her face. She was wearing a neck brace . It was hard. Very hard. Emotions were welling up inside me, and I went over to her, and placed my hand on her arm and called her name out quietly. I knew she was unconscious, but just felt I had to say something. I immediately noticed her breathing was very rapid and irregular. I didn't know what to think, or what to do.

I just stared at her, almost willing her to open her eyes and smile. Of course, I also knew, deep down inside, that was never going to happen.

I was ushered back into the waiting room, where the two detectives were also waiting. They told me Jacquie was being transferred to Hope Hospital for neurosurgery, and what was I going to do? Ride in the ambulance or make my own way to the hospital? I told them I was going to go straight there, in my car. And with that, they were gone.

I made my way out of the department to my car, but just before I left, one of the senior orderlies, a large man with a kind face, he warmly gripped my hand and said, "Good luck and all the best". He said it with such sincerity, that moment has stayed with me, but it also left me thinking what did he know, that I didn't?

CHAPTER 3

I.C.U

I had reached Salford en route to Hope Hospital, but I was lost! This was long before sat nav's, well, it was for me anyway, so I pulled into a side street, stopped the car to grab the road map from the boot. Remember, this was still early on a Sunday morning, the offices and nearby companies were all closed.

There didn't seem to be anyone around, but I had only just spread out the map to see where I was, when immediately from behind me, a car drew up and parked very close to me. Out jumped the two detectives I had met earlier. They came rushing over, firing questions at me. "Why have you stopped here?, you should have been at the Hospital by now, is there something wrong? Have you broken down?" I told them I had lost my way and now trying to find out where we were in relation to the hospital. With that, the two detectives gave each other knowing looks and said, "Just get back in your car and follow us closely, and we will show you the way".

It was only a few months later that it all sunk in as to why they came up to me then. I was, of course, the number one suspect! And they were not letting me out of their sights. We arrived at the hospital ten minutes later.

I rushed to the admissions desk and was told to report to the third floor and to go immediately to the ICU ward. Once there,

I was ushered into a large waiting room. I was informed that Jacquie was already in the operating theatre, that she was having surgery on her head, and would probably be there for an hour and a half.

I sat, and I waited. I waited for nearly two and a half hours. I was impatient for answers, but after what seemed like an eternity, I was then ushered into a small annexe waiting/consultation room, and I walked into four people waiting for me. I sat down, and I was introduced to some surgeons and doctors, including the neurosurgeon who seemed to be in charge. He gently and concisely explained everything to me. "Your wife has had a traumatic injury to the left-hand side of her head".

"She was also losing a lot of blood and we have had to perform two full blood transfusions. The left-hand side of her skull was very badly damaged, but more importantly, a quarter of the left-hand side of her brain was so badly damaged, we have had to remove that damaged portion. She has also sustained serious injuries to her hands, particularly her left hand, to the extent that portions of some of her fingers were missing and her thumb had almost been completely severed".

"The injuries are so traumatic that we are having to continue keeping her in an unconscious state. If she started to regain consciousness, the trauma she would experience could dangerously elevate the pressure in her head and on her brain, which would be counterproductive".

The surgeon then said, " Have you any questions?". I said, "Well if you have removed a portion of her brain, that means that something will not work?". The Surgeon said, " Unfortunately, this could affect her speech, and her mobility, although it is too early to know exactly to what extent". Then he leant forward towards me, and I found what came next quite upsetting, he wanted to explain how different the brain is to any other organ in the body. "If you hit your thumb, we know the extent of the damage, where that damage will travel to, and how long it will take to recover, but the brain is completely different. In your wife's case, with such trauma to the brain, we can't tell how far that trauma will progressively damage other healthy parts of the brain, and we don't know when that damage will stop!". I asked him," How long will it take for her to recover, and in his opinion, how will her disabilities manifest themselves?"

We must know at this stage, as I am asking these questions, Jacquie was a very fit and sporty woman, and was in perfect health.

The Surgeon hesitated for a moment. Then he said, "The best scenario is that she would recover. But she would have problems with speech, and it could well be that she may not be able to walk properly. *If* she recovers, she could be hospitalised for up to six months before there is a chance of her returning home". I said, "And in your opinion, that is the best scenario?" "Yes", he said. "These next few days and weeks are crucial to see how your wife recovers; we simply have to wait". And with that, they were all gone. I was left in silence.

I couldn't stop the millions of questions going through my mind. For example, how disabled would Jacquie be? Would she be able to play with the boys, who she loved more than life itself. It would be soul destroying. I just felt deflated and devastated. I felt so sorry for her. I wish there were something, anything, I could do to help her, but at this stage, just being there with her was all I could frustratingly do.

As I sat there, lots of other thoughts were rushing into my head. What about the boys? Relatives? Friends? School? etc

I would have to contact them all. Tell them all what has happened.

It was like looking up at the the sides of a mountain. The impossibility of it all. I had to keep it all together, for the sake of everyone, especially myself. But just where do I start? I didn't think of it at the time. But I was unbelievably calm, and I started to quieten the thoughts going through my head. I took a deep breath, and I began writing out my 'to do' list. But just before I did, I would have given anything for someone to whisper in my ear, when and where, and in what way, all this was going to end.

CHAPTER 4

Nine Days Later

The next nine days were a roller coaster of medical problems, of emotions, of highs and lows, of successes and disappointments. No two days were the same. During this time, our childminders were simply incredible. They loved the boys since they had helped to look after them from being babies. So the responsibility of the boys, during part of the day, were left entirely in their hands. It was important to me, that they understood, that everything else in their lives during this time was to be kept as 'normal' as possible. Each day in ICU though brought something completely different.

One day I went in, only to be told Jacquie was beginning to recover very well, the swelling and pressure on her brain was reducing, a very positive indication, and that if she continues to improve, the Doctors will start to consider slowly letting her regain consciousness.

Another day I went in, only to be told she had contracted pneumonia, she had a high temperature and they were trying to stabilise her.

And on yet another day, I remember walking in to be confronted by one of her nurses, who said there was a group from a local church who were demanding to sit around her bed to conduct a vigil! But quite rightly so, the nurse told them that only two people were allowed around her bed at any one time and they had to be relatives, it was an important rule that is never broken in ICU.

Then a couple of days after that, something happened that I found to be heartbreakingly upsetting. Since the moment I had seen her when she was rushed into A&E, all the top of the head, where her hair would be, was wrapped up in white surgical bandages, as were her hands, particularly her left hand. On this particular day, I walked in to be confronted by her nurse who explained that they had removed the bandages from around her head and from her hands. Her nurse warned me that what I saw may be a shock? What did he mean?

As I went through the curtains to her bedside and sat on the chair beside her, I understood what the nurse had been trying to warn me about. You see, I imagined when they took the bandages off from around her head, I would see all her lovely thick blonde hair. There was no hair. She was completely shaven. Completely bald. And even worse I could see quite clearly the two long scars meandering across the side of the head, with the suture marks either side and to make it so much worse, her skull, instead of being nicely shaped and rounded, was suddenly horribly misshapen on the left-hand side.

We talk about hair on a woman being the crowning glory in some cases, and so it was with Jacquie, and now suddenly to see all that gone, and in its place, the marks and deformity and scars made me well up and then I cried.

Tears rolled down my cheeks. I couldn't stop them. They just came and came. I recovered a little then noticed her hands, especially her left hand. Remembering that Jacquie had her Nail salon, meant she had lovely hands and beautifully manicured nails. Now her hand had part of one finger missing. And her thumb had been severed to the point where it was just hanging on by a small piece of skin (I learnt later on, this will have happened as she was trying to protect herself from the continuous blows of a large stone her attacker was using to disable and ultimately kill her with).

As the days went on, with it's 'ups' and 'downs', it all became a blur. But for every positive step forward to recovery, there were always two steps back to non-recovery.

On the eighth day as I arrived in ICU, I remember sitting by the side of Jacquie's bed. I held her hand and felt compelled to tell her something. Something straight from the heart. Something I felt strongly she would want me to say to her.

You see, I was convinced she was fighting hard, at trying to stay alive, more than anything, for the sake of the boys. I believe a Mother's love for her children is one of the most powerful and determined physical and emotional feelings in the world.

I can remember exactly what I said, as I held her hand and looked at her. They say the hearing is one of the last senses to shut down, so I said to her. "Jacquie, I want to promise you with all my life, that I will always look after and love our boys, and if you feel you are struggling with life, and want to let go, then you must. It's ok to if you want to move on peacefully, they (the boys) will be just fine, and you will always be in our thoughts". Something changed from that moment. I can't tell you what it was. A 'knowing' if you like, did her hand slightly relax?

I was still around the bed when Jacquie's nurse came through the curtains to carry out some checks. All the while she was chatting, she was reading charts, writing on them, checking the I/V lines, life support machine etc. Then she lifted Jacquie's eyelids one at a time and flashed a little torchlight into them to watch how the iris's reacted. I noticed the left iris only reacted a little and, the right one didn't react at all! I remember thinking to myself, that was wrong, the iris's should react and constrict when a light is shined into them. At the same time the nurse turned to me, and with a smile, she said, "That's all fine". But I knew it wasn't.

A few minutes later I got up and made my way to the large waiting room which was packed with relatives, friends from work and so on. Jacquie's nurse popped her head around the door and gently motioned me to join her. All conversation stopped in its tracks as if we all knew something serious had happened.

I was shepherded into a little private consulting room. One of Jacquie's consultants, who had the main responsibility for Jacquie, wanted to see me. I somehow knew the news wouldn't be good. I waited, then he came in, pulled up a chair, and sat quite close and opposite to me.

He was so gentle in what he was trying to tell me, so sensitive, that at first it never registered what in fact he was trying to say, and he could see that on my face, so he explained again. "Remember, we mentioned at the beginning, how we would never be too sure how far the massive trauma and subsequent damage to Jacquie's left-hand side of her brain would travel to other parts of her brain?"

"I'm afraid to say, the damaging effect of the trauma has steadily continued throughout her brain and has now fatally affected Jacquie's brain stem. To all intents and purposes, we believe Jacquie would now be deemed brain dead! There is absolutely nothing we can do to make her recover now".

"Unfortunately, because she is on a life support machine that is breathing for her and administering all other life-giving functions, including drugs that are necessary for all this to happen, we are unable to carry out the definitive tests to conclusively confirm Jacquie has died and for us to issue a death certificate".

"We have to wait for a full twenty-four hours, for all this to happen, then tomorrow at this time, myself, another consultant and her hospital doctor will be present while we carry out invasive tests to prove, without a doubt, that Jacquie has died".

"These tests are very demanding regarding their severity, and of all the number of tests we carry out, if there is just one positive reaction, we would not be able to conclude Jacquie has died, and wouldn't issue a Death Certificate. It is, of course, your choice whether you would want to be present during these tests. At the end of the process, if *all* results are negative, and she doesn't react at all to any of the particular tests being administered, only then are we able to issue a death certificate, and we will then decide to turn off the life support machine".

"After a short time, once the life support machine has stopped, Jacquie's heart will slow down, then stop". I sat quietly for a moment. It had finally sunk in that Jacquie had actually died.

I knew this time would come; I felt like I was sitting in a bubble, a bubble where time stops, where there is no sound, no forward or backward, just a 'nothingness', not knowing when that bubble will pop.

When the consultant left, I gathered my thoughts and picked myself up slowly, and went back to the larger private waiting room, which was full of relatives and friends etc.

I knew I had to tell them all that I now knew. All eyes were on me when I entered the room. There was absolute silence. They made room at one end, I sat down, and told them I had some news about Jacquie. The boys Godmother, Nanette started to cry, and she was consoled by her daughter. They eagerly looked at me. You could have heard a pin drop, and I was trying my best to compose myself. Although my voice was wavering a little, I told them everything the consultant had said to me. Some collapsed, some just bowed their heads and started crying, others just looked at the floor in disbelief. Then, I suddenly said to my Brother, "Kevin, I just need to get out in the fresh air".

As I left that room, two of the Detectives were there and very sensitively wanted to know the latest news about Jacquie. I simply told them she has died. They turned on their heels and rushed off. It was now officially a case of murder.

CHAPTER 5

Saving Lives

Not long after I had told everyone the news, took in some deep breaths of fresh air from outside the Hospital, I walked back into ICU, and I was introduced to a lovely lady who was a transplant coordinator. She asked me a question, which was, would Jacquie have wanted to be an organ donor? Immediately I said yes! Jacquie and I had talked about this over the years, and typically of Jacquie, the 'giving' person she was, she always said she would want to be an organ donor.

It was explained that in this case, they wanted permission to keep her connected to the life support machine, and then to transport Jacquie to a hospital in Liverpool, an hour away, where they would remove the organs for transplant.

Now, originally, after the definitive results that would confirm that Jacquie's brain stem had died, we would then have turned off the life support machine. A short while later her heart would have stopped, however, in this case, this wouldn't happen until after some of her organs were removed and sent for transplant. (It has to be noted at this stage since Jacquie's death was now officially classed as murder, certain organs were not able to be removed, they may have to be used as evidence, and would need to be present for the post-mortem by both the prosecuting and the defence counsels). To me, someone dies, and especially in Jacquie's case, when the heart stops beating.

After discussing this with the transplant coordinator, she said she would kindly let me know, as soon as Jacquie's heart stopped beating after the organs had been removed and the life support machine switched off. In my mind, this is when Jacquie would have died. Which means, to me, her true time of death was approximately twenty-four hours after that recorded on the death certificate. The Death certificate would say the 8th of February, 2005, but it will always be the 9th of February 2005 to me.

Sometime later, the transplant coordinator also told me that there were initially going to be three recipients of some of Jacquie's organs. Also, her pancreas would be used to produce much-needed insulin. Her liver and both her kidneys were going to three very ill people. Each of her kidneys went to two people who had kidney failure, and her liver to a young man who had a fatal liver disease and very close to death.

I heard nothing for a few months, and it had escaped my mind with everything else that was going on. However, one day a large package arrived from the transplant co-ordinator. Any recipient of transplanted organs cannot contact the relative of the donor directly, or vice versa for obvious reasons, so what was contained in the envelope came to me via the transplant co-ordinator. She told me that two very poorly people were recovering, as a result of each having one of Jacquie's kidneys. Then the rest of the package contained some letters. I mentioned previously that a young man, in his early 30's, who had fatal liver disease. He was very close to dying. He received Jacquie's liver, and now was making a remarkable recovery.

The letters were from him, his parents, his Grandparents and his friends. They were full of generous thanks for the 'Gift of

Life' as they described it. How life is precious, and that they, and he, were able to look forward to a long life. From a simple gift to a lifetime of everything life can offer.

It was at this point, and more was yet to come, that I realised that out of this senseless tragedy, three people were alive today because of it. I ask you, how wonderful is that? Even in death, she was doing what she liked doing best, helping people.

CHAPTER 6

Last Rites

Immediately after I had spoken to the transplant coordinator, and agreed Jacquie would have liked to donate her organs, almost as an afterthought, she asked if Jacquie was a religious person, and if so, what religion was she? Well, a smile did cross my lips, and I said she was a roman catholic, albeit, a lapsed Roman Catholic! She promptly said there was a 'resident' priest, and would I like to see him on behalf of Jacquie and for him to possibly administer the last rites?

I am a Buddhist, a Mitra, who believes in practising Buddhist principles and ethics, and Jacquie had always supported me on the religious journey I was on, so naturally, I said I would like to meet him very much. The transplant coordinator said with a wry smile " He is lovely, but try to imagine a British version of the American movie star, Mickey Rooney". I couldn't wait to meet him after that.

An hour later, into the waiting room came this small bundle of energy, with flapping black robes and a beaming smile, and introduced himself as the priest. He was so lovely, with a slightly wicked sense of humour, and began asking me all sorts of questions about the life of Jacquie.

But before all that, I felt I needed to tell him straight away that I was a Buddhist. I just felt it was important. He stopped in his tracks, came up to me, held my hands and said slowly, with a very concerned look on his face, "Well Michael, we can't all be perfect!". And with that, his beaming smile came back, and we laughed. He asked permission to administer the last rites, and of course, I agreed. He asked if I would like to be present, and I said yes. And so he started the ceremony. When he reached that stage where he said to Jacquie, " Jacquie, I absolve you of all your worldly sins". I couldn't help smiling. You see, in my mind, I wanted to say to him, don't forget those drinking binges we used to have on Gran Canaria, where we used to go BC. (before children), and at that precise moment he glanced around at me, and of course, I had this silly grin on my face, and he asked if everything was alright? I told him the story; then he continued with the little and beautiful ceremony. I am so pleased I agreed to all this, especially for Jacquie.

Afterwards, as we were walking away, he was genuinely sorry for what had happened, and his sincerity and compassion was absolute.

But just before he popped into the lift, he turned to me and said, "As long as those drinking binges bring back thoughts of your love and companionship and happiness for Jacquie, then you hold onto them Michael, precious memories, never to be forgotten. You and the boys will be just fine, and Jacquie would be so proud of you all!"

CHAPTER 7

The Boys

I must explain that Jacquie and I had two boys, Ben and Oliver. However, I also have an older son from a previous relationship. Aidan and I met Jacquie when I was single with Aidan. Aidan was around one year old, and to all extent and purposes, Jacquie was his 'surrogate' mother, took to him immediately, and loved him very much. I didn't realise at the time how difficult at times that must have been for her, but luckily, we all got on very well, and Jacquie, Aidan's mum and myself, always put Aidan's welfare first. This was eleven years before Ben and Oliver came along.

When Ben and Oliver came along, we always talked about them all being brothers, no difference between them all, and that is how it is to this day.

What I am going to mention now, is out of context, but to me very important, since it is very relevant to Aidan and myself, and happened when we learned that Jacquie was diagnosed as having died.

Referring to that moment towards the end in the I.C.U, when I had been told by the consultant that Jacquie had died, and I then went into the large private waiting room to tell everyone who was there.

Moments before I went in, I asked Aidan if he would please

wait in a much smaller waiting room annexe. I just felt I wanted to tell him privately. Just the two of us. I just felt the impact could be so overwhelming, I wanted to be the only one there to help him, so that I could give him my full attention. Up to this point, I had not broken down, in many ways I suppose, I was preoccupied with everything happening every day.

So I sat opposite him, we brought our chairs close together, and I faced him. I started to tell him, as gently and sensitively as I could, what had happened to Jacquie, and that she had died, a slightly scaled down version of what I had just told everybody else fifteen minutes earlier.

I was just coming to the end when I suddenly felt emotionally overwhelmed; tears were rolling down my face, I found it hard to speak, and taking in long sobs and crying.

I remember putting my hand on his leg, and bowing my head down, and with my forefinger and thumb, pinching the top of the bridge of my nose. I was trying to say sorry for breaking down like this, and the last thing I wanted to do, was really upset him, by him seeing me like this.

I stood up then and looked at him. He looked at me. He came to me almost immediately, he was now beginning to cry and we stood there for what seems an eternity, hugging each other tightly, both of us crying uncontrollably.

That moment of absolute openness and emotion will stay with me forever. And, in retrospect, an important cleansing, and emotional releasing stage for both of us. (Many years later, we were talking about this little incident, and what had a huge impact on him then, was the fact that in front of him was his Dad, strong, thoughtful, loving and always in control, and now *not*, but very upset!)

Oliver had just had his fifth birthday party a few days before

Jacquie was attacked, and Ben was six.

Although it was incredibly busy, with trying to run our two businesses, coping with the start of the murder trail etc. my mind was on so many things that were happening; however, I made two decisions regarding them. Do my very best to protect them from the graphic nature of the high profile news, which seemed to be everywhere. And two, to try my level best to make life appear as normal as possible for them and ensure I was there to love them as I always had done, and even more importantly, that someone *they* loved, and who loved them, was around.

Of course, there were news reports in the national newspapers and on television, which I was protecting them from, but that didn't mean I didn't tell them about Jacquie. I explained that their mummy had been knocked down by a horrible man and that (in those early stages) she was in a hospital, and the doctors were looking after her, trying to make her better.

They did ask questions, which I answered in the kindest of ways. Sometimes, they didn't seem to want to know things that I thought would be important. So I didn't pursue this. I partly assumed, some questions they knew the answers to already, and so on. I just felt that if they felt secure, loved and cared for, in their home environment, then that would be the best thing to do.

Of course, the help, advice and involvement of the boy's childminders (a husband and wife team) was invaluable. So much so, I was quite happy with them dealing with the day to day activities, which they did gladly.

I always made a point to get them dressed and off to school, and most times picked them up, but tea time, bath time and bedtime, was my time with them. (The childminders were so much a part of the boy's lives since they were born, it was an easy decision for me to make them official guardians if anything should happen to me following Jacquie's death). There was something I came to realise very quickly. We have so much to learn from children. It's sometimes difficult to comprehend that we were all children ourselves once.

At the beginning of all this, Oliver was still in nursery school, where it seemed the rest of the children had no idea what had happened to his Mum, and of course, they would be unaware, they were very young.

For Ben at Junior school, it was a different kettle-of-fish, even though he was in the reception class, the other children were more aware of what was happening. They had heard their parents talk; they may have seen newspapers and TV reports, etc.

I remember one day going to school to pick up Ben, who was in reception class. As I walked in, a little boy came up to me, tugged on my trouser leg, looked at me and said, " Ben's Mummy is dead isn't she?". The boy's mother came over immediately, full of apologies, but I understood, this is exactly how children are. Learning the social niceties comes in time, but this is the honest truth, something else I wish we didn't lose as we grew up into adulthood. Straight to the point, with no emotion, very matter of fact. Ben was with me when this boy said that, and he and the boy went off to play quite happily.

The school were amazing. The Headmaster couldn't have been more helpful and understanding, and offered a route via his office to the reception class, instead of waiting with every-one outside the school gates. Ben decided to accept that, and so we did that for around a month. Then one day Ben said he would like to go through the school gates, just like everyone else, and that's what we planned to do the very next day.

That morning, I'm there with Ben, on the other side of the little side road opposite the school gates. All the other mothers were there with their children, and they immediately noticed us.

The school gates were opened and in poured the children. I kissed Ben, hugged him, and told him I would see him later. But when the children went in, most of the mothers were still there on the other side of the road. Some of them had not seen me since it had all begun, and all knew Jacquie. Those that didn't know me, now did of course. And as I saw them, I had this distinct feeling that they wanted to come over to talk to me. Inside it made me smile. It was like looking at the start of the 1500 metres at the Olympics. They were shuffling around, looking at their feet, whispering and glancing at me.

Time to take the initiative I thought, I stepped forward a few steps and said, " It's ok you know? I won't bite! It would be lovely to say hello". And with that, one by one they came over to say how terrible it all was, was there anything they could do, and invariably they became upset and started to break down and cry. So I simply hugged them and told them it was all ok. After the sixth or seventh Mother came over, and this scenario had repeated itself each time, I said to everyone, with a gentle smile on my lips, " Erm, have I got this all wrong? Am I not the one who is supposed to be breaking down and crying on *your* shoulders?"

Very quickly, I realised this was something I had to be prepared for, friends and especially relatives, didn't know how to deal with it all, and certainly not with the children or me, so I constantly had to take the initiative. And that, at times, was incredibly difficult. And by that, I meant, having a relative just sitting in front of the children and breaking down constantly in a flood of tears was not very helpful for anybody, especially the boys.

I was urging all of them to try to move on from that area of grieving, and of course we all had to grieve, and there are numerous stages of grieving, but there were certain things that I believed we needed to keep foremost in our minds, for example, taking our leads from the children and moving and dealing with things that were happening in the present.

I remember another time, around a month and a half after Jacquie was murdered, that our oven and hob had broken down, irreparably! We needed a new one, and so on the next available Sunday, which just happened to be mothers day, we all went to a big superstore to purchase a new, all singing, dancing hob and oven. There was a smartly dressed middle-aged lady who was very helpful talking about and demonstrating the models. I chose one pretty quickly, and I was filling in all the reams of paperwork when Oliver came up to me.

Immediately the sales Lady kneeled down and asked Oliver what he had given his Mother for Mother's day. He stopped, looked at her and said,"Oh, my Mummy is dead and she is an angel in heaven" and with that, he skipped off to play with Ben. That poor lady, burst into tears, desperately apologising, still kneeling down on the floor where she had spoken to Oliver. "I didn't know. I'm so sorry". And of course she didn't know, so again, I gently picked her up and comforted her till she had composed herself. The boys had noticed this and Ben asked me, "Dad, why was that Lady crying?". But of course, they were oblivious to what had happened.

I will be discussing the police in depth in a later chapter, but for now, it's important to know I could not fault the police in any way, shape or form. They were helpful beyond belief, and they told me pretty early on, that there were resources available to me, at no cost, that I could call on if I felt I needed help in some way. Of those resources, there was a family therapist and a child psychologist.

Going back to the end, at the ICU. It was decided Jacquie's injuries and trauma had meant that eventually, her brain stem was dead. The hospital had to leave it for a full twenty-four hours before carrying out the definitive tests to confirm this, in the presence of a consultant and two doctors, where they then signed a death certificate. These tests were carried out on a Tuesday, but on the Monday, I knew the end was inevitable, so I decided the Tuesday afternoon would be the time I would tell the boys.

On that Monday evening, I decided to phone the family therapist. I wanted to know the best way of telling the boys their mother had died, and what I could expect. So I spoke to a family therapist. She knew exactly who I was, and what the situation was, and I asked her the questions. She told me, I didn't need to separate them, but tell Ben first, which I did, in the gentlest of ways. She said he would probably react as an adult would and become upset, so be there to comfort him for as long as he needed it.

Oliver, she said, would be completely different, simply because of the age he was, his development age, and that when I tell him, expect a different sort of reaction, or even no reaction at all. In any case, she said, and particularly in Oliver's case, I needed to make sure there were photos of Jacquie all around our home, and we continue to talk about her as much as possible, which we do still to this day. The reason for this, she explained, is that children of that developmental age could easily forget they had a Mother figure at all.

So, first of all, I told Ben that a horrible man had hit Mummy on the head and hurt her very badly. That the hospital had been working very hard to help her, but the damage was so severe, she had passed away peacefully and was now in Heaven. He asked me a couple of questions which were, "Was she in pain? Was her head hurting?". And quite truthfully, I said no, she had not been in any pain from the beginning. (Since she had been induced into a coma from the moment I saw her in A&E until she was removed from life support)

He thought about this for a moment, then broke down and cried. He sobbed and sobbed, and we held each other very close for what seemed an interminable time. Then he composed himself and just sat looking at the floor.

Phew! That was very hard for both of us. But I held it together.

And now I had to tell Oliver. I sat him on my knee, cuddled him, and he seemed to understand I wanted to say something important to him and told him a slightly scaled down version of what I had told Ben. I said to him, "Is there anything you want to ask me?"He sat quietly for a moment.Then he jumped off my knee and grabbed my head, looked straight into my eyes and said, "Can I play on PlayStation now?".

I am so glad I had phoned the Family therapist, I really wouldn't have expected that sort of reaction.

Helen, the childminder, offered to be with me when I told the boys, and I gladly accepted. I trust Helen implicitly, and couldn't have thought of a better person to be there. The boys were certainly more comfortable with Helen than anyone else I knew.

As time passed, Oliver by now had moved up to junior school. He had his obligatory photos in his new crisp, clean uniform, that seemed two sizes too big. On his first day in reception, just like all the other Mothers, I admit I shed a tear, not just for the fact he was growing up, but that this was one of those moments in every Mother and Father's lives, that is special and needs to be remembered. Jacquie should have been here, but I am sure she was smiling down from above.

I was also beginning to get in touch with my 'feminine' side. By that I mean, that if one of the boys fell and grazed a knee for example, I just wouldn't tell him to be brave, stop crying and pull himself together, I would sit him on my knee, cuddle him, and whisper into his ear, wipe away his tears and tell him that he would feel better very soon.

Now, there were questions that the boys asked me, but the majority were not to do with their mother or the future, but other mundane things like "What are we having for tea?" etc I would like to think, that many of the things they had wanted to know, I had already answered for them, and I certainly didn't want to put questions into their heads, but six months after Jacquie had died, there was one question that did keep surfacing. It was a question that both Ben and Oliver wanted to know the answer to. And it was a question that they both, in their ways had discussed among themselves, and it seems every time they asked it, both of them were there!

"Daddy?, when will you die?". So this was it. The million dollar question, and quite understandably, they wanted an answer to this one.

If their mummy had gone to heaven and wasn't around, then the next most important person in their lives was me. So far I had filled Jacquie's gap to a certain extent, and as I have mentioned before, here was the other half of the partnership that will always love them, and they didn't want that taken away.

How was I to answer this? I'm always for truth and honesty first of all. But I believe you can say the truth in a gentle way, that isn't too alarming. And if they could see that I was approaching it in a gentle relaxed way, it would put them at ease a little. I realised if I didn't handle it well, it could well be a recurring little thought that would keep popping up.

So, very simply I said to them, one day I will go to heaven, as will you, and I reminded them of the story of the car, that the body of the car finally, after many years, gets old and rusty, and can't move anymore, but the battery, with the living spark, never dies, and that battery may be put in another new car, and that new car will drive around for a long time.

So it is with me, I'm still a nice shiny car, well, pretty shiny, with a good battery, and there is no reason why I shouldn't be driving around for many years to come, but sometimes accidents do happen of course, but the chances are rare. And they were happy with that and accepted it wholeheartedly. They stopped asking that question again, and it hasn't been asked of me, thirteen years on.

By now though, my head was full of thoughts of the police, the looming murder trial, the press, our hair, beauty and nail salon businesses.

I was preparing myself, as best I could, for all these things that were lining up to fall on my lap, or most probably, onto my shoulders.

CHAPTER 8

The Press

Jacquie's attack had made, not only headline news on all ra-dio, and television networks, but was the lead story across the board in every journalistic article, or so it seemed.

In those very early days of the police investigation, I met the police press liaison officer. It was quite clear she wanted to warn me what to expect from the press, particularly the well known national tabloids, especially with such a high profile incident as this. She warned me that they would try every means possible to get information on myself, on Jacquie and the boys. But they wouldn't stop there! Relatives, friends, staff at the two hair, beauty and nail salons we owned, some of the clients, our neighbours where we lived and even our ninety-nine year old next door neighbour.

No one it seemed, would be spared a visit to get the tiniest bit of information, no matter how small. But it was the lengths they would go to get that information.

The attractive female journalists, who knocked on my door, in short, skimpy attire, who fluttered their eyelashes and were full of false sympathy, would try to eke themselves into my liv-ing room. Coincidence? Nope, I had visits like that from four female journalists from the same clone factory.

I came home one day, to hear a little knock on my back door.

It was our ninety-nine year old neighbour. She told me in her frail diminutive voice, how two separate ladies had managed to get themselves invited into her cottage, where she duly offered them tea and biscuits. "We would love to know all you can tell us about Michael and the boys", said the journalists.

The urgency by the press for information very quickly became intrusive.

I was being called now by friends and relatives and staff complaining about this, so I had a word with the police press liaison officer, and she said she would arrange a meeting with the press to try to come to some arrangement.

Around a week later, we met up, and she told me I had a choice. She wouldn't be able to stop them pursuing anyone that knew us for information but would work to just within the press commission guidelines. That this would continue until the end of the murder trial, or, they would leave all of us alone, as long as I agreed to give a full-blown press conference immediately following the result and sentencing of the murder trial. This I accepted, it just wasn't fair to our friends and staff at work to be aggressively sought after for information, and after that, in fact, the press did keep their word.

Now, just as the press were very intrusive with their investigations, in doing their best to get information, it seemed as if there was now a 'working relationship' between the police and the press. They were 'working' together to try to find the perpetrator of this crime. The press agreed to put out information appealing for leads that may help the enquiry, in return for the police making available information on the case that they felt was right and proper and lawful to disclose. I am convinced that the press releases in those first two weeks of the incident were very helpful for our case.

Also within those first two weeks, I was shopping in a local supermarket when my mobile rang, it was a journalist working for one of the major tabloids, who I had spoken to earlier, who wanted to interview me at that very moment.

So for the next, almost forty-five minutes, while I am shopping, I am being interviewed in depth. I was slightly oblivious to the stares of other shoppers who were looking and listening to this one-sided conversation. It must have sounded very unusual. And I must say, there was nothing sensationalist about the piece, it was well written and can see, it's what people would have wanted to read. In fact, I was even emailed a proof before it went to press.

I also had lists and articles in some of the country's leading magazines such as Closer etc. in fact, it was this magazine that had sent a journalist up from the South. She was pleasant, making all the right sympathetic remarks, but it was her reaction to something I said when we were in my living room, looking out from our bay window. You see, from our window, there is a magnificent vista, over-looking the Strines Valley, but you can quite clearly see, on the other side of the valley, to the right, a wooded area that hides the Peak Forest canal, where the attack took place. You can also see, above the canal and centre, the road the murderer ran up, and the side street he ran to his parent's house.

When I told the journalist this, she was visibly shocked. She immediately said, "How can you continue to live here? Are you thinking of moving? How can you look out at that view, with the horrible thoughts and memories of what has happened there?". When she finished, as we were still looking out, I said to her, "Well, first of all, this house is our house, where the boys were growing up, where there will always be lots of happy memories. When you look out at that view, it all depends on what it is you are looking for".

The journalist replied, " What do you mean?","Well, I said, there are two ways to look at it, and you are quite right, one way is to look at the sights and the reminder of what has happened, but I'm not like that. And this doesn't mean I am trying to bury the horrible thoughts, and that then they will fester away and cause problems for me at a later date".

"No, I said, (pointing across at the valley), I'm genuinely looking at the beauty of the place, the trees, the old Roman viaduct, the wonderful old sweet factory, the green rolling hills. And especially the happy memories we all had as a family when we would walk through those woods in the valley at various times of the year". At the time of writing this, I regularly look out at the view, and take in and appreciate it's beauty.

Going back to the newspaper reports, it wasn't long before I found out, that all anyone needs to do, is Google search 'Jacquie Ross New Mills' and there are all the local newspaper reports from the time. There is nothing I could do to have that re-moved, even if I wanted to, and I guess will still be there long after I have gone!

CHAPTER 9

The Police

It was a policeman who first answered the mobile phone on that fateful Sunday morning that suddenly confirmed that something had happened.

Then there were the detectives I met at A&E in Stockport, who later came to assist me when I was lost in Salford trying to find hope hospital where Jacquie was transferred for brain surgery. For the nine days, she was in the hospital, they had an unobtrusive presence, waiting for any news on what was happening with Jacquie.

It was quite clear now, they were also there to know if Jacquie was going to die as a result of her injuries, because then the case would immediately be upgraded to murder. In fact on the day I was told Jacquie had died, I passed on the news to the police, who sped off with the news.

Of course, since day one, they had been working very hard to find the perpetrator, but now it was murder, this escalated the resources, manpower and finances right away. We had to find the person that committed this crime. The first two weeks of a crime of this nature, everything is put into the investigation, manpower, finances, but they were desperately working on a strict timeline and budget. After this, the resources and finances start to be drastically cut back; time was of the essence. From the beginning, I was introduced to the detective superintendent and detective inspector who were in charge.

I was also introduced to a police family liaison officer, Jenna, who over the coming months proved to be invaluable to me. Both as a supplier of information of everything that was happening with the case, the breakthroughs, the disappointments etc. but probably more importantly, she was emotionally very comforting for me. She was always available and always so helpful, and I needed someone who I felt was on my side, but not obtrusively, or officially so.

Both She and the Detective inspector would regularly visit me in my cottage to discuss the latest developments with the investigation, and, when the murder trial itself began, Jenna would always drive me to the crown court in Chester, and back afterwards.

It's worth noting here, that within the first few days of the case I was driven to Macclesfield police station to have a DNA swob (let's not forget, I was also a suspect, initially the prime suspect, and needed to be eliminated from the investigation).

While at Macclesfield police station, I was told that the team were working round the clock to find clues that would point the finger at a suspect. I felt humbled that all these people that didn't know me personally, and were working very hard on my behalf. I asked if I could just meet them all briefly to express my thanks. I was led into the incident room, which was a lot larger than I had imagined. It was a hive of activity, people rushing everywhere, computers, papers, phone calls, but the Superintendent asked for everybody's attention.

Immediately it went quiet. Everyone looked at me. The superintendent introduced me and said I would like to say something. I simply said how very grateful I was that they were working so hard on this case, around the clock it seems, for a positive result, and I would like to thank each and everyone of them. You could have heard a pin drop. There were smiles and looks of appreciation. As I left, the hubbub of activity started off again.

I have always believed that everyone should be shown appreciation if they have put themselves out to do something for you, in fact, in my mind, it's much more important than offering a criticism.

Over the following months, Jenna became an important part of our lives, in fact, eleven years on, and Jenna is a close and lovely friend, and we occasionally meet for lunch and a catch-up.

Thanks to the press and the diligence of the police, and the offer of clues from the criminal fraternity in the area (you see, even criminals have a sort of code of conduct and to cold bloodily murder a woman with two small children did not fall within their ethical code) they were very close to catching the suspect.

Very soon they had reprimanded a youth (who was just under twenty-one years of age, was known to them and belonged to a criminal family). As more details about him became known, it became more upsetting.

Here was a person that found violence towards women was something that he enjoyed, that 'turned him on', and was revelling in the fact that he had been let out of prison half-way through a four-year sentence for a previous crime he had committed. Historically, he had walked into a pet shop and bitten the head off a hamster, had desecrated a church, and ran the occupants of a Chinese take away out of the area with violent intimidation, to name just a few of the terrible crimes he had committed.

Serious and huge mistakes by the probation service had meant that the movements of this criminal were not instigated and set up as they should have been on his release from prison.

And so this attacker was waiting on the corner of the Peak Forrest canal, early on that January Sunday morning, after a drug-fuelled night of alcohol, for the first innocent and vulnerable woman to walk passed. And that innocent and vulnerable woman was Jacquie.

I very quickly learned, that by the use of police investigations, and the use of cutting-edge technology etc. the prosecution counsel, were very quickly able to piece together a moving time-line picture of what had happened.

There is an area of the canal which is on a long slow bend. There are lots of trees and shrubs on both sides of the bank. The murderer was waiting in hiding on a section of this bend. There was a loose excuse for a wire fence, (3 lines of metal wire stretching from one small concrete post to another, to prevent anyone falling on to the other side, away from the canal, and down a steep embankment).

And it's on this bend that Jacquie and our dog Rosie (a soft coated wheaten terrier) would have been confronted by Ben Redfern, the murderer.

The defence counsel would later claim that Rosie attacked Redfern and that he, in his defence, hit out accidentally knocking Jackie over the fence, and he would run off. And they continued to claim it was then someone else that attacked Jacquie. This was pure fabrication on behalf of the defence counsel.

Our dog Rosie had always been the gentlest of dogs, always pleased to see people, never barked at anybody, but gladly welcomed them, even absolute strangers.

In fact, what had happened was, when all the evidence came to light, and from admissions from Redfern at a later date during the trail, as Jacquie approached him, he grabbed her violently, and pulled her over the fence and dragged her, whilst hitting her over and over again, to a level section that was at the bottom of the muddy embankment.

Now, as it was explained to me, and to remind you, here was a person, who was turned on by violence to women. He was young, very strong and tall, so physically, very intimidating. His initial thoughts were he was going to rape Jacquie, once he had subdued her with a constant onslaught of violence.

It was explained to me by the police, that the majority of women, in cases like this, where an attempted rape is in progress when confronted by so much violence, tend to let themselves be raped rather than be badly beaten and fatally injured.

But we now know, Jacquie did *not* want this to happen. She fought back as hard as she was able to. He had managed to pull her tracksuit bottoms and panties down, but she was still fighting back. He now needed to subdue and silence her even more, so he grabbed a large stone to hit her hard, violently hard, across the head and face. All the while she was trying to protect her head from the constant blows that were raining down on her using her hands. She was crying out for help and shouting out to him that she would recognise him, and that he would never get away with this.

The accused, from evidence submitted later during the murder trial, confessed, he didn't want to go back to prison, so he decided to rain these hard, aggressive blows, with this large stone, to Jacquie's head, again, and again, and again, until she was barely conscious and bleeding profusely, then ran off back to his parents house.

Shortly after this, it was a dog walker with his dog, walking along the path, and he spotted a dog's lead and a red leather glove on the path in front of him, he looked around, then over the make-shift fence and thought he saw a movement at the bottom of the muddy embankment and went down to investigate. What he found at the bottom of the embankment, was awful, a memory that has affected him very badly since, and from which I was spared. The shock of what he saw in the mud and dirt of that spot, he says, will stay with him forever.

At first, he couldn't tell it was a man or a woman, there was so much blood everywhere, all over her head and face, and then he noticed the tracksuit bottoms were pulled down to her knees, together with her under garments, and suddenly realised it was a woman, and immediately turned his head away in embarrassment. He would say she was only just conscious and was trying to speak, but couldn't do. "Blood was bubbling out of her mouth, and she was trying hard to speak," said the dog walker.

He ran off to a nearby farm to raise the alarm, since he wasn't carrying a mobile phone and waited for the police and ambulance to arrive. All this all took time because of the remoteness of the area where the attack took place.

In fact, later on, as with all police investigations, it was given a name, which was 'Operation Remote'.

CHAPTER 10

The Murder Trial

The Police informed me that they now had someone in custody who they believed was the chief suspect, and with the evidence they had, he had now been officially charged with murder. The murder trial was to be conducted at Chester Crown Court. The police offered to transport me to the Crown Court and back every day if I wanted them to.

To be honest, as the months went on, it became more and more harrowing, so fairly soon into the trial, I elected only to go in when I felt there was a witness, or evidence that was being admitted, that I felt was important to see or hear.

On day one, I was introduced to the prosecuting barrister. I felt assured our case was in good hands, and he explained, in detail, the workings of the court, how the responses and questionings had to be presented, that the judge would expect courtesy and how it all had to be conducted in a particular manner, that I might find a little strange, that the judge would listen and make notes from both the Prosecuting counsel and Defence counsel.

There were delays and even mistakes! For example, Jacquie's body would need to have a post-mortem conducted by the pathologist's under instruction by our prosecuting team, and when finished, the body would be then presented to the Defence counsel who would conduct their post-mortem. This all took time, particularly in the fact that the Defence counsel's team, messed things up, and they had to call in another team to conduct the post mortem, so yet more delays.

This all meant, and most importantly to me, that there would be longer delays before I could have Jacquie's body for the funeral and memorial service. Because of these delays, it was approximately six weeks after her death that Jacquie's body was finally released, when then I could put into plan the funeral and memorial service arrangements.

One of the key moments for me, and this may sound strange, was I wanted to see the murderer in the flesh, to hear how he would respond to the questioning.

I wanted to understand the events that led up to her attack, what the perpetrator did next. How he was helped by his Father, to try to dispose of evidence, to see the large stone that was used to bludgeon her, at the time, to within an inch of her life, to understand what was it in the mind of a murderer that would make him do this.

It wasn't long into the trail that a doctor I knew, said to me, "This person isn't wired up the same way everybody else normally is, and that you may not find any rhyme or reason for his actions".

Five months into the trial, as a family, we had a holiday booked in Gran Canaria, and I decided not to cancel, but to go, and this is covered in chapter thirteen.

The first time I saw the murderer, Ben Redfern, was when he was brought into the courtroom. Since he was classed as a category one suspect, the witness stand was surrounded by plate glass on all four sides, with little one inch to two-inch gaps running from top to bottom on the corners. To me he looked

ugly and seemed to show no remorse whatsoever. From his attitude and body language, I could tell he didn't seem to care one
iota.

We were all sitting in the top gallery of the court room facing
the judge, with the murderer in the dock to the left, to his left
were the detectives. To their left and further up were the press
gallery which was full, and I noticed one of the blonde haired
reporters that had been pursuing us all for information. I caught
her looking at us, not smiling, expressionless, seemingly making
notes.

Directly in front of me on the left-hand side was prosecuting counsel and to the right was the defence counsel. There
were some steps leading up from the middle of the court from
the basement, where there were presumably holding cells.

Six months into the case, there were times when all the jury
and court officials were transported to the scene of the crime,
to survey the area, and so nothing was happening in court.

One day in court, the prosecution introduced a large stone,
that was used to bludgeon Jacquie across the head. It was in a
clear plastic bag, a misshapen greyish stone with blunt and
sharp edges to it. As I saw that stone being passed along from
jury member to jury member, I found that very upsetting.

It's worth noting at this stage, after all the investigations by
the police, after all the information, orally and technically, had
been gathered, the prosecution had a clear picture of what had
happened, from the very beginning to the very end, when the
murderer went on the run, including timelines and so on.

After Redfern had completely disabled Jacquie, leaving her
for dead, he then ran along the path, up to a side road towards
his parent's house, covered in blood where his Father made him
strip out of all his bloodied clothes, which were put in a black

plastic bin liner bag. The Father then raced to the municipal tip and disposed of his shoes and clothes, knowing this would be the best place to dispose of this vital evidence. He then took his son to a friends house to lie low.

There was lots of other evidence, such as CCTV footage of Redfern buying alcohol from an off-licence the night before the incident, ready for his night of drinking and drug taking. There were footprints at the scene of the crime, and the police were able to determine the size and make of the trainers. (He was wearing trainers in the CCTV footage in the off-licence). He had unusually large feet. And so with blood samples, DNA etc. and later information from the criminal fraternity in the area, the police now had a good case and went to find and apprehend him, which they did.

During the days I attended court, there was obviously due course and court etiquette, and when either the defence or prosecution asked a question, the question and the answer seemed to be all hand-written down by the judge. I remember thinking, please get on with it! There were so many breaks like this; there didn't seem to be any continuity to it all.

All sorts of evidence was submitted, for example, the clothes she was wearing, all jewellery, her backpack, and even her mobile phone.

Her phone was almost brand new, pink and sparkly, but a lot of time was spent on it, gathering information from it, in particular, every single person who was a recipient of that number on her phone was investigated, and everyone questioned until the police were able to conclusively clear them from the investigation.

It was explained to me, that if the prosecution didn't fully investigate every single person on that phone, and eliminate them completely from the investigation, then the defence would, and may try to suggest that one of those, on the phone, may have somehow had enough connection to be possibly responsible for Jacquie's murder, thereby clearing their man of being accused of the crime.

Since Jacquie's phone was virtually brand new, I wanted to have it back but was told I couldn't for many reasons, the technicians, in their investigations, had taken the phone apart completely, so they could swab everything inside for DNA. (It is thought that Redfern may have picked up the phone, to silence it, on the many occasions I was phoning it and making it ring), and also, that they would find it next to impossible to re-assemble it, and secondly, it would have to be kept in permanence as one of the exhibits, and securely stored indefinitely. The same happened to some of Jacquie's jewellery, including a lovely gem stone belly button piece of jewellery, which I had bought her as a present once.

There were also times when the defence lawyer was calling a prosecution witness a liar when we all knew the witness wasn't lying, the defence barrister was doing his best to convince the jury that his client was not the person who committed the crime. Their alternative arguments, were beyond belief, with no substance to them whatsoever. They were claiming that someone else had committed the crime and that Redfern had come along and by pure chance had found Jacquie, had gone down the embankment to try to help, which is why he was covered in her blood.

The defence barrister was very eloquent and did make convincing arguments, and at times I wanted to stand and scream out that none of what he was saying was true.

And so we came to the end of the trial.

The prosecution and defence had made their closing statements, and the jury went to retire to make their judgement.

It was at this point that our barrister made me aware that no matter how convincing our case was presented, and that he should be found guilty on all counts, with the evidence and arguments made, you never really know the outcome until the jury pronounce their decision. He did say, the longer a jury deliberates, then that can mean unwelcome news, because the jury may be undecided on which way to cast their vote.

To wait for the jury to make their decision was very difficult. It seemed I was counting every minute, trying my best to calm myself. This was the culmination of nearly a year from the incident, to finding the person who committed this crime, and finding them guilty. We had a call to say, in just over two hours, the jury was ready to give their decision.

We took our seats back in the courtroom, I had my Brother Kevin and other relatives and friends and of course by my side also, as she had been from day one, Jenna, the police family liaison officer.

The jury came in and took their seats. I noticed some of them glancing up to where we were sitting.

The judge asked the jury foreman if they had reached a decision, to which the foreman said, "Yes". "Please, will you inform the court of that decision", said the judge. The Foreman took a deep breath, looked up at the judge and said: "We find the accused guilty on all counts". For a second there was silence, then all those around me, punched the air and shouted out "Yes! Yes! Yes!"

We all had tears in our eyes, but what happened next was quite shocking. The murderer in the dock turned around to us, looked straight at us, flicking 'V's at all of us, and mouthing the words "Fuck Off".

As two policemen started to restrain him and take him away, he managed to get his mouth to one of the corner gaps of the security glass box he was in, where the detectives were sitting and started violently spitting at them, through the gaps running up and down on the corners, and swearing at them! I remember thinking, I hope the judge is watching this. It was around two weeks later that the judge would pass sentence.

When that sentencing date came, the murderer was given twenty-two years. I questioned this with our barrister, who explained that because the murderer committed the crime as a 'juvenile' (he committed the crime a day or two before his 21st birthday) for some reasons, it was the maximum the judge felt he could give.

In any case, it was explained to me, it was almost irrelevant, because he already was showing signs that he would not be able to integrate back into society, plus the defence counsel would have objected, and there could even have been a re-trial and for it to be conducted down in London!

Almost thirteen years on, I do get regular updates from the probation service, and since those times, he is deteriorating socially to such an extent, life to him will mean life, and he will never be released into society.

Finally, there were some 'firsts' with this case. A full record of the incident, including photographs, were to be kept on file by the probation service, if he could possibly, in the future, be presented before a parole board to consider his release. There could be a parole board twenty years down the line, who may not have known about this trial, but in this case, they would be presented with all the evidence to study, including photographs. He will never be in a position to be considered for parole, but it is somehow comforting that all the evidence is there, and would need to be read and examined.

At the very end of the case, and I was told this was unprecedented, the judge asked if I was in court? I stood up right away, but he waved me down and said, " On behalf of the court, I wish to offer my condolences to you and your family".

The judge also had in his possession, my 'impact statement' that the judge was required to read, to explain how this all had affected my life, the lives of the boys and my relatives. There came a point at the end of the case, where the judge read out some of the impact statement to the court.

In all, I tried to explain, that to me, one vital thing was missing, and that was 'fairness'. It simply wasn't fair that Jacquie had been taken from us, that she would never be there for all the times in a Mother and her children's lives that are so special, like the first day at school, when they get married, when they get their first job, first car, the birth of grandchildren and so on.

The murderer received 22 years, but I argued that myself, Ben and Oliver received 'life sentences' for having a wife and Mother taken from us. Another worrying aspect of this whole affair were the rumours that started to surface about Jacquie and the murderer.

What is it with people, particularly those that we don't know, somehow wanting to try to find a tenuous link as to what had happened. It's as if the simple motive and truth were not enough. Ok, so with that in mind, the rumours were built up on here say. Lots surfaced, and it seems they all had an underlying theme. The most common one was that Jacquie was a witness to a crime she had seen him commit once, and gave evidence at a trial at which he was convicted. So, go the rumours, he wanted to 'get her back'.

Another time, my second in command at my hairdressing salon, popped across the road to the florists to buy some flowers. There was a middle-aged woman in front of her that was telling the florist, that she knew Jacquie and me very well indeed, and indeed, Redfern had committed the crime as a pay back for Jacquie being a witness, and that there may be many other rumours, but because she knew us so well, her version was the absolute truth!

When my second in command stepped forward to question the woman, she asked her, "She has two boys, do you know what they are called?" She spluttered and stuttered and then said that she didn't want to divulge their names to just anybody. And after some other pertinent questions, it was quite clear this woman did not know either of us in the slightest.

I still can't quite understand why people do this. Is it to feel important? Do they have self-esteem problems? I quickly became dismissive of all the rumours that were flying around. I knew the truth, and that was fine for me, and I promised myself, I wouldn't rise to anything I heard. It simply wasn't worth it, there were much more important matters at hand.

CHAPTER 11

The Press Conference

Immediately following the end of the trial, we made our way to a nearby hotel where the press conference was to be held. I was led to a little room and there met Detective Inspector Rumney and a representative of the probation service. Also, there was Jenna Timmis, the family liaison officer, and the prosecuting counsel and some more police.

I couldn't quite understand it, but I felt very calm. However, the probation service head was very nervous, and rightly so, they had made some gross mistakes regarding not knowing the whereabouts of Redfern on his release from prison, considering his past record. There were questions that needed to be answered as to why Jacquie's killer had not been monitored as he should have been.

On the other side of an adjoining door, which would lead to a much larger room, I could hear many voices. We waited by the door ready to be ushered through it.

Suddenly it was opened, and myself first, then Detective Inspector Rumney and the probation officer, walked into a much bigger room that was packed to the brim with journalists, reporters and video cameras, either hand-held or on tripods. At one end was a long desk with three chairs, and behind it, as you see all the time on news reports, a white three-part standing backdrop. We sat down, with me in the middle. I took a deep breath and looked up at all the expectant faces.

All of them were looking at me, searching my face for some sign of emotion, trying to gauge my composure.

I believe that experiences in your life can sometimes prepare you for events that are to present themselves later on in life. I have always been a professional actor, and somehow, the training as an actor to feel calm in a situation, that was quite the opposite, came to the fore.

The first person to speak was a reporter. He introduced himself by name and said he was with News at Ten, and after passing on his condolences, proceeded to ask his questions, followed immediately by others in the room. I remember thinking quite clearly, all of them in that room I felt were being very sensitive to my situation, respectful, and for that I silently thanked them. The questions came quite quickly and were straight to the point, I can't remember Inspector Rumney being asked many questions, and the probation officer only one or two, the majority were directed towards me.

"How are you and the boys coping?"," What were your thoughts now towards the person that was found guilty of this crime?". To this question, someone else asked, on the back of this "Do you think you could ever think of forgiveness?", I found answering this question very easy. I replied by saying "I am not the one who can forgive him, only one person can do that, and that is my wife Jacquie, and she is up in Heaven".

"How did you feel the Police handled the whole investigation?", "Were you satisfied with the sentencing of only twenty-two years, and able to accept this as life?". And it was this last question that really got to me. I knew what I wanted to say, but for the first time, could feel my composure wavering. I just knew it would be difficult to say out loud what I was thinking and knew I would have to fight hard with every word to not break down. It was all welling up inside me. "Yes", I said, "He was sentenced to twenty-two years in prison, and it has been explained to me why it is only twenty-two years, and not life, but I just find it all just simply unfair!

Unfair, because he could be out in twenty-two years, but I will never see my wife again, and the two boys will never see their Mother again". (We now know it is very unlikely he will be released!) "But it just doesn't stop there, I continued, we have to remember all those key points in our lives, that will now be missing as the boys grow up, whether it be as a Father or as children, for myself, the pleasure you get as a family, as the children grow, the planning of our businesses, which were coming along so well, will now all be missing".

"And for Ben and Oliver, not having their Mother at special times in their lives, first day of school, sports days, passing a driving test, birthdays, getting married and so on. No, it's not just twenty-two years for us, we will be serving 'life sentences'! And that's why I say it's unfair". Then suddenly, the press conference ended.

At this point, I remember thinking , this had been a hell of a journey so far but was yet another milestone that had been reached, and it was now, that I realised I would need to begin to start to put some thought into how we were going to put all our lives back together. Up to this point I had been in overdrive, my over-riding sense of responsibility, towards me, the boys and so on.

I had constantly been working hard at trying to keep it all together and was able to step back a little and be, for want of a better phrase, pleased with how we all were all doing at this stage. At the same time, I also was acutely aware that without the constant pressure of dealing with the police, the court case etc, suddenly, with all that out of the equation, I had time to think about everything else now, and just hoped I would be able to address the problems and issues that were bound to present themselves over the next few months and years.

But the now over-riding satisfaction I did get from all this, is that the person who attacked and murdered Jacquie, had been caught, sentenced and he was now behind bars for a very long time.

CHAPTER 12

The Memorial Service

I had to wait just over six weeks before Jacquie's body was released, so that we could have the much-needed funeral and memorial service.

In a murder case like this, the body has to be available to be examined both by the prosecution and defence, and as mentioned earlier, very annoyingly, in this case, the first pathology team the defence employed to examine Jacquie's body, apparently were replaced by another team. All this meant that time was running on and on.

A funeral is very important to me, because, before it, I have always felt like I was in no-man's-land. For my father, aunt's and uncles, grandparents etc. the moment a funeral has come to an end, is the point of closure to me. It's a very restless time just waiting for the funeral to take place, and so when I was informed that finally, I was able to have Jacquie's body, I knew that after it, I would be able to begin to start putting our lives back together. I didn't want a full-blown funeral, and since I am a Buddhist anyway, wanted something a little lighter. To celebrate Jacquie's life, was the overriding priority.

Also, not forgetting the boys, I believed a memorial service would be helpful for them, but attending the funeral and crematorium would not. My thinking here was based on my child-hood, in that when my grandfather, whom I loved dearly, had died, his body was lying in waiting in my grandmother's living room. I was only twelve. My mother ushered me in, forcefully, to say my last 'goodbye's' to my grandfather, but standing in front of him, and seeing this lifeless grey looking, cold, greasy body, with no life or warm personality, no breath, I found very upsetting and shocking, and that vision has stayed with me until this day. Why, oh why, did my mother force this on me? I could have quite easily remembered him with photo's and stories, without having my nose pushed into the 'adult' idea of having to be with and seeing the body, such was the way in those days, to ensure closure and respect.

And so I decided that there would be a simple funeral, and immediately following that, a memorial service. As far as the boys would remember, the service was a celebration of all the good and happy times, but also a confirmation that she has passed on. In my mind, a gentler, much less traumatic way of doing it. And the result? Even now, the boys fondly look on the memorial service with thoughtful memories of a beautiful, warm, loving Mother, not a cold grey body in a coffin, with horrific injuries that caused her death. The boys would not ac-company me to the funeral, but I would pick them up en route to the service. Waiting six weeks for Jacquie's body was more than enough time to arrange the funeral and the memorial ser-vice.

The funeral was in Macclesfield and was a very simple affair, even so, the little chapel was packed, with faces I recognised and others I did not.

Somehow to me though, and of much more importance, was the memorial service at a large church, St.Georges, in New Mills where we lived.

The plan was to arrive back at home, after the funeral in Macclesfield, where the boys had been looked after by my childminders, Helen and Edwin. As we were waiting for the funeral cars, Oliver and Ben suddenly came up to me shouting that "The Men in Black are here Daddy!". And sure enough, they noticed the long black funeral sedans, that had parked outside our cottage, the funeral staff in black suits, white shirts and black ties, and because it was sunny, wearing dark sunglasses!

I had been working very hard over the past few weeks to make this event as special as possible. A friends husband played in a Jazz quartet, and they agreed to play 'Give me Sunshine' when everybody was walking out of the church at the end. I had also insisted that everyone, please wear something colourful, we were celebrating Jacquie's life and didn't want it to feel so oppressive. I knew that the church was going to be at full capacity. And that was approximately four hundred and fifty people.

My eldest son, Aidan, had even composed and produced a beautiful song, 'Best Things In Your Life' which he also performed during the memorial service. (The lyrics for this song may be found on page 111). Another friend of Jacquie's, very kindly put together a soundtrack of songs that were to be played, but it was the first song, right at the start of the memorial service, that set the wonderful celebratory and thoughtful mood. 'A Hundred Thousand Angels' must have caught the hearts of everybody in that church.

Now, a week or so before, when I was preparing the order of service, I was explaining to Ben (who was six years old at the time) where the songs were going to be played, who I had asked to stand and say a few words about his Mummy, and so on. He suddenly said to me, " Daddy, I want to say something as well!".

That caught me by surprise! I asked him if he was sure he did? Surely a six-year-old was bound to be overwhelmed if he was suddenly to face four hundred and fifty people! I said that I would help him compose something pertinent and simple if it would help? He said. "I know what I want to say", and with that, he was gone.

Well, ok then, I didn't know what to expect, and I suppose looking back on it, I was probably more nervous for him and what he would say than anything else to do with the planning. I was not sure if he would break down when halfway through his little speech, or if he was even able to start on it, so I made the decision to be right behind him when he went up to speak.

And so it came to that point in the memorial service, when the vicar asked Ben to come up and say what he wanted to say. I was right behind him, ready to jump in if necessary. Well, I just wanted to be there to help and support him. He slowly got up, went to the little microphone on a stand, facing the whole church and said, "My Mummy has died and has had to go to heaven, she wouldn't want us to be sad, she would want us to be happy and to smile". For a moment, there was absolute silence, you could have heard a pin drop, and after a moment or two, we made our way back to sit down.

Later on at the wake, lots of people came up to me and said they wanted to stand and applaud Ben, but out of respect for the church they didn't. But that moment stayed with everyone who was there.

I had asked some people if they would like to contribute by way of a little speech on their memory of Jacquie, which they all agreed to, and one was a very close friend of mine, a leading Buddhist, and he said he would love to say something. I remember seeing him just before the service in a little panic, being a simple man, of few possessions, he realised he didn't have a tie, so we sorted one out for him.

Because we knew the church had to be a large one for lots of people attending, I had a very close friend who was a minister at a local United Reform church, but that church was tiny, so she asked permission from the vicar of the much larger church in New Mills, St. George's, if we could use his church, to which he agreed immediately.

Now, when I told my friend, the minister from the united re-form church, about who was speaking, she noticed I mentioned a Buddhist. She suddenly became anxious. She was wondering what he may say, would it conflict with normal Christian teachings, and more importantly, because she felt responsible for 'borrowing' St. Georges's, felt responsible if something was said that might conflict with Christian views. She expressed her concerns to me.

Immediately I told her to meet my Buddhist friend, have a coffee and a chat, and see how she felt about him. Sometime later I caught up with her, she had a big smile on her face, "What a lovely gentle man he is, I am perfectly at peace with what he is going to be saying".

It was my turn to say something. I took in a deep breath, I slowly scanned everybody there, and the feeling of warmth was unbelievable. I thanked everyone for being there, mentioned that within the tragedy there was also hope and life and that in many ways, it hadn't all been for nothing.

Another remarkable thing about that memorial service was that it brought sections of the community together, even factions within families that had been distant for one reason and another, so yet another positive effect.

But now it was over, and although the murder trial had only just begun, I felt a weight lift off my shoulders. I was so proud of all my boys, their composure, their attitude, and more than anything, I felt very pleased, and I do believe this very much, that Jacquie would have been very proud of all of us. And as Ben said, she would be looking down on us all with a big smile on her face. To me, it couldn't have been better.

Something happened a few days later after the memorial service. Pope John Paul II had died, and in the national press and on television, they published one of the pope's last speeches before he died. What was remarkable, was that almost word for word, part of his speech, gave the same message that Ben had written for his a few days earlier. I know it could be argued that it was coincidence, but what a lovely thought.

That night, I had my first uninterrupted nights sleep since it all began.

CHAPTER 13

The Holiday

Jacquie, myself and the boys had booked a two week holiday the year before, for July 2005, staying at the Princess Hotel in Playa Taurito, Gran Canaria. With everything that had happened, I had decided initially to cancel the holiday, but the more I thought about it, I decided it should go ahead.

I needed to know that I could organise it all from beginning to end, that I could take two small children away on holiday, bearing in mind, Oliver at that stage still was in nappies at night. Also, I needed a breather, and it could do nothing but good for the boys and myself, some sunshine, warm weather, swimming pools, and more than anything the change of scene and my mind on other things, etc. The murder trial was, by then, in full swing, and I had decided right at the beginning, I only wanted to attend for, what I would call, the 'important' stages, ie introduction, summing up, juries decision and other relevant witnesses and so on.

It turned out to be a holiday of mishaps, and fun. It was a hotel that we had holidayed at already, even before the boys had come along. I was familiar with it, and so were the boys.

If you were on holiday and noticed a single man with two small children though, would you be curious? Curious in that you may wonder, where was the Mother? We as human beings are naturally curious, and so, I could tell questions were wanting to be asked.

Now, what a mother would do, is not ask me why the boy's mother was not there, that would be rude. Instead they would, in a roundabout way, when collecting their children, and the boys would be playing with them, ask the *boys* where their mother was. To which they answered, she is an angel, and she is in heaven. So one by one, a mother would come to me and say how sorry she was to hear about Jacquie, and if there was anything they could do to help, I only needed to ask.

In fact, one woman, who was a childminder here in the UK, came to me one day and said, " Look, why don't you have a day to yourself, and I will look after the boys for you". They were all very kind, hearts in the right places, and very soon I made some lovely friends.

I am, and always have been very open, and a number of them already can remember that Jacquie had made the headlines six months earlier, and I filled in the details for them with everything that had happened. As I explained everything that had happened so far, I would have a group sitting in front of me, not saying a word, listening intently. Afterwards, after a thoughtful minute or so, they remarked with things like "I don't know how you are coping", "How terrible", " You must be a very resilient person inside", and so on, but more than once someone would say to me "You are such an inspiration".

Now, it was that that overwhelmed me, I just did what I did, did what I thought was right, for myself and the boys. To be patted on the back with 'Well done!" really was unexpected.

What all that did for me, was to suggest that what I was doing was right and going in the right direction. I mean, there were no books then that would take you step by step through the grieving process, for a man in my situation, and how to live each day as it comes, by doing this and that.

Half way through the holiday, one evening, I was sitting with around a dozen friends I had met, around the swimming pool. It was around eleven pm, and all the children were playing just inside in a games room which we all could see.

A waiter came up to our group and called my name out. I put my hand up, and he came up to me and said there was an urgent telephone call for me from my brother Kevin.

I rushed upstairs to our room and picked up the phone. "Hi Kev, what's up?". He seemed upset on the other end of the phone. I asked him, "Whatever is the matter?". He said, "Dad died this morning, he had just finished having a dialysis session at the hospital, and had a heart attack and died".

I let out a very long drawn out sigh. Could it get any worse?. But you know what? I was very calm, and already was trying to help Kevin organise the funeral etc It may sound very strange, but I had thought of how I would start the eulogy at my Fathers funeral, and I replayed this to Kevin, I said, "If Dad has ended up somewhere, as hot as it is out here in Gran Canaria, he has gone down to the wrong place!". We both giggled at this, our Father had a wicked sense of humour, and I imagined him chuckling at this as well.

After another fifteen minutes of trying to sort out arrangements, I went back down to my friends and took my seat. They all looked at me expectantly, and asked if everything was ok? I said, " My Father died this morning". There was silence, a shaking of heads and comments of "We are so sorry" and so on.

In retrospect, I am so glad we went on that holiday, even though, it seems, I couldn't escape more bad news, it was a change of scenery, a chance to meet new friends and the boys and myself were all the better for it.

Finally, we come to the end of the holiday, and I thought we had said our goodbye's to everyone we had met at breakfast time.

I had arranged a taxi to collect us at eleven o'clock. We packed everything up and waited at the front of the hotel for the taxi, and as we walked through the foyer to the front, I noticed around fifteen or sixteen people also waiting at the front of the hotel?. They were all the friends we had met. "What are all you Guy's doing here?" I asked, "Are you all leaving as well?". "No" said one, "We've come to say goodbye properly of course".

We hugged and shook hands, and again they were saying how inspirational I was. Honestly, this took me aback. I was genuinely overwhelmed, and as we drove away, and they were smiling and waving, I did get quite upset then, and to think that less than two weeks before, all these people were strangers to me, and suddenly I felt we were all very close. I have kept in touch with many of them since that time. And although sadness played a part, with my father passing away, I will also have fond memories of that holiday as well.

CHAPTER 14

The North Face of the Eiger

In Switzerland, there is a mountain called the Eiger. It's a stunning looking mountain and one side of it is the infamous north face. It is steep, enormous, imposing and intimidating.

From the very beginning when Jacquie was found, and I first knew what had happened, until a few weeks after the murder trial and press conference, to say my mind had been occupied, was probably an understatement. I didn't have time to think about what I was going to do now, both for myself and the boys. And so it was, when I had time to take a breath, the full realisation of what had happened finally hit home, and I could think beyond the necessities of day to day living.

I had to think of the future. And it was then, that it felt like I was looking up at the north face of the Eiger. It was daunting, frightening and scary as hell, because I had no idea how to start, where to go and what to do.

But then I remembered two things. One was an old Maori proverb which states, "When you dare to have the courage to stand and face the sun, you will find your shadows fall behind you." I liked that, I understood that and I applied it to my situation.

Secondly, I remember listening to a mountaineer friend of

mine once, talking of mountains he had conquered, and how, even though everything had been planned and researched, that first look up at the difficulty and steepness of a mountain could take your breath away. It would make him nervous, anxious and even, at times, want to run away and hide, although it had all been planned for months in advance. So what he did initially, was not to look at the top of the mountain, but look for that very first foot or handhold that would lift him just off the ground.

Immediately that put into motions two things. He suddenly had started, and he was now nearer to the top. He realised then that the second handhold and step were now possible, and each time he was reaching ever nearer to his goal. This gave him the confidence to move onwards and upwards.

And so I took on board these useful tips and tricks, and they have proved to be invaluable, and continue to be so.

CHAPTER 15

Destinies & Help

I believe that all our life experiences from the moment we can remember, have helped shape us, and help us to deal with problems with which we are confronted. In that respect, I count myself as very lucky. So far I have had a very varied life, and the experiences from all these aspects have helped me cope, confront and move on.

I spent eight years at Boarding school from the age of eleven. My parents lived and worked, for much of that time, in Nigeria, West Africa. It was the boarding school that made me independent. To face up to life in general and try to deal with them. The mindset was there as soon as a problem arose, to face up to it, and do my best to deal with it. It was gaining my experience of life in, what some would call, a harsh way, but in my case, would turn out to be very helpful.

I also became a Buddhist in my early 30's, not an ordained Buddhist, but a Mitra. Someone who believes in living his life within Buddhist principles and ethics. And it was one of these principles that would turn out to be the most helpful to me and would help me not only wanting to move on but finding the emotional 'tools' to move as well. A major principle is that of 'non-permanence'.

What does that mean? Well, one day, you, the chair you are sitting in, the clothes you are wearing, the room you are in, the house or building you are living in, one day will not be there. The realisation that something would not be around for ever had a powerful message. It certainly did for me.

You see, when I took that first breath after that news conference at the end of the trial, everything had to change. I was now not preoccupied with the day to day running of the trial, the press, the constant updates and meeting with the police etc. I felt permanently bogged down, that I was on my own, and nothing would ever change, but suddenly, to my rescue, came the idea of non-permanence.

So, if I believed that everything moves on, no matter what it is, then these dark memories, feelings of helplessness and being stuck in a rut, also had to move on. That, coupled with the hope of positiveness, was my saviour.

Music, for example, has always been a big part of my life. I had been playing the piano since I was seven and all the way through boarding school, and little did I realise that at times during the murder trial and afterwards, there were times I felt drawn towards the piano, just to play, to lose myself in the music. I now know that was the instrument of my therapy. (Strangely though, I also play tenor sax, and with that, I just couldn't summon up the energy or even the breath to play it.)

I remember one time, I had a hard day in court, I came home, and Aidan was at home. I went upstairs and sat at the piano and started playing. I was beginning to get upset. Aidan came and sat on the stool with me, and I stopped, and we just hugged for ages, and then we played for a long time as well, not uttering a single word!

Oh how it helped, unbelievably, to enable me to lose myself, and come out of a session feeling as if a heavy weight had been lifted off my shoulders.

There were also I guess, coincidences, which I cannot explain, that afterwards, somehow seemed to make sense.

I mean, why was it, two weeks or so before Jacquie died, she explained in detail how to wash the boys school trousers and shirts. Don't misunderstand me, I am a very practical man, I can cook, shop, clean the house and operate a washing machine etc. but this was very specific. I can remember very clearly, even now, how she explained how I could wash the boys trousers and shirts on a low wash, spin well, shake out and hang on the old fashioned ceiling clothes maiden we have in the kitchen. When they were almost dry, to tumble dry them for a short time, take them out shake and fold, and that meant I did not need to iron them!

Not long after Jacquie had died, I felt I wanted to explore groups that were out there for people like me, that had gone through similar experiences, not necessarily where a partner was murdered, but certainly where a partner had died and someone was now left with a child or children. I can't remember if I was given a lead, or I had searched it out, but a charitable organisation was put on my lap.

WAY (Widowed and Young). This organisation was there to help people like me. And my main reason for pursuing this was to meet and talk to people that had experienced similar tragedies. And in particular, that hopefully there would be contact on an empathy basis. Of course, they had experts who technically knew how to face up to and start to overcome problems with loss and grief for example, but there is something very special and empathetic in chatting with someone that has been through a similar situation to yours. And indeed, I found this to be the case. I was able to talk to someone, in detail, about the problems I was facing, and vice versa, knowing that they would understand. WAY seemed to be the only organisation, at the time, that would seem to fit what I was looking for, to help me move on.

Sure there were others, but they seemed to be bent more towards helping older, retired people, that had lost a partner, and where possibly no children, were involved.

There are a number of other excellent organisations as well nowadays (you will find a list at the end of this book with contact details) who were maybe not around when Jacquie died, or I had not heard of, like Grief Encounter, Winston's Wish and Child Bereavement UK.

WAY was a godsend for me, and in the early days, I did find them helpful. Once registered, and they checked credibility, there were area coordinators, and you had a list of members for those areas, with contact details and a brief description of their circumstances. Remember, this was all volunteer work, but the area coordinators would arrange meals out, meetings at other members houses, a visit to a show, a dog walk, and so on.

It was helpful, but as I started to move on, I found it more and more difficult to continue my membership. Because, for someone in the early days, thoughts and emotions are very raw, and once you move on, it can be difficult, and in my own experience, found it was holding me back as I came to terms with everything. So after three to four months I left, but I need to reiterate, the organisation was invaluable and very helpful for me at first. There were also meeting or dating sites, particularly for widows and widowers.

I guess I started to think about my life once the trial was over, and was beginning to think of possibly looking for someone, more than anything, as a companion. My wife had been taken away from me, and I never thought I would be in a situation where I would want to try to find another partner. And so it was, I came across a widows and widowers dating site one evening. I started to trawl through all those that were in my area, then started looking further a field, and couldn't seem to find anyone, for various reasons, that I felt I would like to meet up with. So, I clicked on the London section. I did this because they had hundreds of women in London, compared to the provinces, and also, at the back of my mind, I thought if I did meet someone, I could always use the excuse of distance to call it off, if I wasn't entirely happy.

And so I came across a profile photo that caught my eye. She looked very attractive. She was younger than me, had a husband that had very sadly died of a heart attack, and left her with a boy and girl who were more or less the same age as Ben and Oliver. I composed a simple message but deliberated for what seemed like an eternity, before I pressed the 'send' button. As soon as I did, at first, I regretted it, and I couldn't think why? (it would all become clear later though).

I waited and waited. Then a message came back. A lovely message, bright, bubbly, polite and I began to get an inkling of her personality, which immediately I warmed to. Our messages then started coming thick and fast, and what I particularly liked was the humour that was bantering between us. When I filled in my profile, I said I was a widower with two boys; I didn't mention how Jacquie had died or the circumstances surrounding it.

What happened then was, and quite rightly, this Lady decided to check me out, see if I was bona fide, because even sites like this can attract the wrong sort of men, who feel they can prey on women who are vulnerable. So she managed to find the newspaper reports of the murder and the trial. She then messaged me to say first of all, she apologised for checking me out, but then how sorry she was to learn of our circumstances, and if I wanted to break off contact with her, because she had taken it upon herself to check me out, she would understand. Hmmm. This now made me want to meet her even more than before. I liked the honesty; it was very reassuring.

We made our first phone call, which is always strange, because you know a little of someone after messaging for a while, but to hear a voice, with possibly an accent, some days or weeks later can throw you off, as if you have to get to know that person from a different angle. When we telephoned each other, the calls could go on for one or two hours! Then we met for the first time, and that again was a mixture of emotions. And each time we messaged, then met, at the back of my mind I felt uneasy, and I still didn't know why?

It bugged me. I needed to have an answer. Then one day it suddenly came to me. So I had a wife, and I believed in the sanctity of marriage. Then my wife was taken from me. And now I found myself on the verge of an affair and realised what the stumbling block was. This may sound very strange to you. I felt like I was being unfaithful! How bizarre! As if Jacquie was around somehow, and I shouldn't be doing this. I was in effect feeling guilty! I mean, it wasn't as if our marriage had broken down, or we were going our separate ways, or I didn't love her.

So I talked to myself, gently and logically, and told myself, that what I was embarking on, was first and foremost a 'friendship', natural, right and should be fulfilling, and could lead to happiness, and with that, without being selfish, we both were able to move on.

Our friendship grew and grew, and we always generally met with the children as well and even seeing the children playing happily together, with them knowing that they too were in similar circumstances. This was all helping to cement our friendship.

We helped each other in every which way, to come to terms with everything our circumstances were throwing up and helped each other tremendously when problems arose with our thoughts or with the children. Meeting up, as we did, was singularly the best thing I ever did and was definitely part of the healing process. I would not be in this happier settled place for me if I had not have pressed that 'send' button right at the beginning.

Michael Ross

CHAPTER 16

The Clairvoyant

Ok. So you either believe in clairvoyants, or you don't. Jacquie and I both went to see one, every blue moon. Three months after Jacquie died, I felt drawn to go to see someone.

Sure, I was hoping I could get a message from Jacquie, or at least, to be told something about her. I didn't need to think of where to go. It was a woman I had seen only once before, and that was over six years previously. What I had liked about her then, was that she was not what I would call a 'guesser'. In other words, in those cases, the reading would run like this. "There is a tall man here from long ago, he is wearing a uniform, could be blue or grey, and his name begins with a 'P' or an 'A' ".

Well, not this lady, not this clairvoyant. There was no guessing involved. She would look you in the eye, and come out with facts. Specific facts. She wouldn't go into a trance, she would chat with you, and she would record the conversation for you, so that you could play the tape back later. In fact, this is just what I did, and I made a transcript of the conversation, and these extracts were taken straight from the transcript. I promise I have not elaborated or made up anything of which I am going to tell you.

So, one morning, at eleven o'clock, I knocked on her door. She opened up and said, "Hello, it's Keith isn't it?" I told her I wasn't called Keith, but Michael, to which she smiled and replied that it didn't really matter. We went into a medium sized living room. There were jos sticks and some Buddha figurines but essentially looked just like anybody else's living room. It was quite well lit with natural light, and the ambience seemed perfect. I was booked in for an hour. She sat in a chair set at a slight angle to mine. She had a tape recorder on her lap and started off with a short prayer, then she looked at me and said: "Let us begin."

She pointed out that I could stop her at any time to ask questions, and that she may repeat certain points, only so that I would know I needed to understand the points being made.

And so she started. For the first half an hour, she talked all about me, how I am the proverbial horse in the field, how one of my hooves was stuck in the mud, but now I'm beginning to free that hoof. And she could see me flying in the air now, like an eagle, that I would experience a freedom that I had never experienced. Hmmm! I never interrupted once but was feeling a little frustrated because I wanted to find out if there was any connection with Jacquie.

Suddenly she stopped. She was very quiet as if contemplating and looking over my shoulder, then she said, "A beautiful blonde woman has walked in, she is holding out a bun, not an ordinary bun, but one with currents in it, and she is offering it to you!. She is offering it to you because she is telling me, you need a little sweetness in your life at the moment.

And now she is grabbing me by the shoulders, and shaking me, and her face is close, and she wants me to tell you something very, very important.

She is telling me to tell you, that the way of her passing was very traumatic, and it's this which is very important, and I have to get it right for you, that she is now, totally and absolutely at peace!". That remark hit me like a sledgehammer. It was what I wanted to hear of course, but how could the clairvoyant have known that and what to say?

She went on."She's laughing now; she's laughing at you, she's laughing because you always used to take things the wrong way. She wants me to tell you, that you are a clown!" To this, I just grunted with a smile on my face. She was, of course, right. "What she means is that your face is painted with make-up like a clown, that you are hiding your emotions underneath and you are sad, and she doesn't want you to be sad."

The clairvoyant went on to mention Ben and Oliver, and the fact that we had introduced my ancestor's names as middle names, *and* she named them! How could she have known that?

The rest of the reading brought other interesting facts to light, but at one point the clairvoyant stopped. She went very quiet. And then she started to get upset, and began to cry softly? I wasn't sure what was happening! Then she turned to me and said, "The love she has for you and the boys is overwhelming, very, very powerful, and she will always be there for all of you. It is the depth of that feeling of love which made me react the way I did; it is only a good thing. She is telling me now that those beautiful memory boxes you have each put together of items of hers are lovely, but again she wants you to realise that material things are good, but what is most important here, is her love for you and the boys, and that will last forever."

The clairvoyant went on to say that Jacquie was a very wise spirit, she is teaching in some great halls of learning, but will always be with the boys and me.

Finally, the clairvoyant went on to say, "She is laughing again, and wants me to understand enough to tell you what it is, and why it's making her laugh. She mentions an old small brush or toothbrush, she used to clean something near or around your toilet, and you used to tease her about it, but she says you are doing it now, does that make sense?".

Oh yes, it was crystal clear! Our toilet in the bathroom had brass hinges on the toilet lid and seat, which used to get covered in verdigris, that green colouration that you can get on brass. Jacquie used to keep a little old toothbrush under a panel in the side of the bath, and bring it out every so often, and brush those hinges to make them sparkle.

It was the perfect tool, and I used to pull her leg about it all the time, saying that she had taken being house proud to a whole new level. Well, the clairvoyant was quite right, after all that, I was indeed, using that toothbrush to clean those brass hinges!

Finally, the clairvoyant told me, "whenever I feel a little sad, she will be there to help you remember a happy thought, you will feel a warmth, you will giggle, and that will be her helping you".

When the reading had finished, I came away feeling that the whole world had been lifted off my shoulders. There was a spring in my step, and a true sense of hope that we would survive and pull our life back together. I was absolutely convinced Jacquie's spirit lives on, and she is always around us, helping us.

CHAPTER 17

Children

I am going to write something now that is irrefutable. We were once children! Oh, how I wish we could still think and act like children for certain problems that arise in our adult lives. There are so many good things about children, which for one reason and another we slowly lose as we grow into adulthood. Could I have coped as well if I didn't have the children to look after, love and listen to? Hmmm. Good question.

Don't be sad if you are left on your own with children, because I have found, they helped me so much, and don't ask for a lot from you! The whole world around them can dissolve, but as long as they are kept in the same routine, and loved unconditionally, by someone that has always been around them, they will thrive and be fine. As adults, we can go way over the top, and it can be frightening to them in many ways. We can be overprotective; we can cocoon them in mourning rituals, day in, day out, year in, year out, bringing to bear on them the uncontrollable anguish and hurt that we as adults have. The children don't need this, they don't want this, but they don't know how to tell you.

I'm not saying they should be prevented from mourning, what I am saying is, we all have our ways in coming to terms with it all, and if a child seems only to want to mourn for a week, then that's fine. Always be there to watch and listen.

I used four markers each and every day with the boys.

1. Are they sleeping well?
2. Are they laughing and playing with the other children?
3. Are they coping and continuing to be happy at school?
4. Are they making friends and adapting to life?

Let's take adults; it could be grandparents, or very good and close friends and even cultures. They don't know what to do, how to react, how to mourn other than that is what is expected, and I found I was the one having to set the agenda. It's all about moving on. It's all about living life to the full. It's all about the wishes of our dear departed. Ask yourself this simple question, what would they want?

So let's go back to how I started this off, two very important things. To love them unconditionally and keep to a routine they are used to. These certainly worked for me.

There was an incident at school involving Ben approximately three months after Jacquie had died. The headteacher called me into his office and told me that Ben had started to be very disruptive in class, which was very unusual for Ben. He quickly went on to say, did I want to make an appointment with a child therapist etc. (The police had arranged all sorts of help, free of charge, at a moments notice, that I could call upon) And that, in his opinion, maybe the whole situation was hitting him hard, and his disruptiveness was how it was externalising.

Well, I thought about this long and hard. I tried to think about this not as an adult, and not necessarily as his Father, but from Ben's perspective, so I told the headteacher, that in the first instance, I would have a private chat with Ben and ask him what was bothering him.

That evening I did, and I immediately understood the problem and to suggest to the headteacher, how to cure it. In Ben's classroom, the school were adopting the regime of having some of the desks pushed together, so the children were all facing each other in close-knit groups. What they had done in Ben's case was seat him next to a very troublesome school bully, who was making his life hell and taunting him about having no Mother. The next day I told the Headteacher this and asked for the troublesome boy to be moved elsewhere, which he was, and immediately the problem dissapeared.

Now, I'm not that stupid. If I thought I needed expert help to sort out psychological problems the boys were experiencing, then of course, I would set the treatment in motion, but in the first instance, I listened, not just as an adult, but as a child, then I would act on that. So one last time, try to remember, routine and unconditional love. Keep it simple. And listen, really listen.

CHAPTER 18

Remembering

Quite a few times I have been asked, how do you and the boys remember the loss of Jacquie? This is an easy one to answer. I explain I couldn't see the point of remembering the day she had 'died', because associated with it are the horrendous memories of how she was found, how she suffered, the trial and so on, even for me.

So right from the beginning, I decided we must remember Jacquie, by associating with all the good times we all had together, and in particular, particularly for the boy's sake, I focused on her Birthday. Celebrating her Birthday would be a fun event, full of happy memories. I would buy some flashy helium-filled novelty balloons. We would then make our way to the little open cemetery. The boys would write or draw on small pieces of tin foil a birthday message, which we would tie to the long ribbon on the bottom of the balloon. (We used tin foil pieces because we found that card would sometimes weigh the balloon down, and one time, one of the balloons was caught in the branches of a nearby tree)

We would all then clean Jacquie's headstone, place new flowers in the little pot on top of the headstone. Then, we would all sing happy birthday to Jacquie, and then let go of the balloon ribbons, and the balloons would rise into the sky.

I really can't remember if there was ever a dull day on her birthday, which meant that we were able to see the balloon for a long time. The boys were convinced the balloons were going straight up to Jacquie in heaven. (If the wind was blowing in the right direction, I'm sure the balloons would have landed on the east coast of Ireland)

Another way to remember Jacquie was to talk about her, look at photographs. To this end, our cottage is filled with photographs of Jacquie. Then there are the videos of all of us as a family. This would light up the boy's faces.

Something else we would do, when decorating the Christmas tree in December, is to put our favourite photo of Jacquie right at the very top of the tree, where the fairy would usually go.

We also have the memory boxes. Each one of us has our own, and in them may be some perfume, some lipstick. (This was important to the boys because, if Jacquie and I were ever going out at night, leaving them in the hands of a babysitter, Jacquie would tease them by trying to smother them in 'lipstick kisses'. In fact, 'lipstick kisses' is engraved on her gravestone.

An article of clothing , shoes, some jewellery, her favourite CD's, lace gloves etc, are just some of the other items found in the boxes.

In every room of our cottage, we have a photo of Jacquie somewhere. I put together a large photographic collage which has photos from when we first met, (some of which have been used in the design of the cover for this book), to the birth of the boys, when Jacquie and I married and so on, that we could refer to if we wanted to.

Another question I am asked lots of times is, do the boys talk about Jacquie a lot? To which I reply, no, not a lot, and immediately a worried look crosses their faces. I have to explain, to me, the fact that they *don't* mention Jacquie *all* the time is a healthy situation to be in, in fact, if they did talk about her a lot, it's then that I would start to worry.

To me, if they only mention Jacquie every blue moon, then it tells me they are happy and adjusted. They have come to terms with it all in their own way and leads back to what I have already mentioned earlier on. If they are loved and cared for by someone who is close to them, and an integral part of their world and daily routine doesn't change much, then they will be happy and content.

CHAPTER 19

A Little Thought

I think the hardest part of losing someone, isn't having to say goodbye, but rather learning to live without them. Always trying to fill the void, the emptiness, that's left inside your heart when they have to go.

It's a little like looking up at the night sky full of shining stars, and up there, somewhere, is a little smudge of blackness.

So in that little smudge of blackness, try to fill it with memories. With happy thoughts, with music, a gentle caress, a sweet song, and soon you will find you can't see that little gap anymore. Because those special memories will fill that gap, and the other stars will then snuggle closer until that smudge of blackness is a thing of the past. You will never forget of course, but you will feel it has been addressed. All the other stars know what you are going through, and so they are there to help you and support you. And it will make you smile, and you will start to remember the good times, but most importantly, it will help you to keep moving forward, to appreciate life and live it to the full.

There is so much that living and life has to offer, you must try to accept it as a gift, knowing deep down in your heart, your loved one would honestly not want you to be upset, they would urge you to accept your gift and be happy. But of course we are only human, and there will be times where you will feel like you have been hit with a sledgehammer!

Here is a little secret! Be gentle with yourself. Be kind to yourself. You are allowed to have bad days, as well as good ones, but more than anything else, the moment you learn to love yourself again in all the grieving and darkness, is the moment you will recognise the love in others, who have always wanted to help, and those dark clouds will start to blow away!

Boarding school ensured I was very independent. This has its helpful, and it's unhelpful aspects. One of the great things it did for me, was to give me the courage to face up to problems and I did my best to deal with them, however, a downside was, that at the beginning, I would say, "No" to anybody's help, whatever it was, and whoever was offering it. Every time I refused. I felt I didn't need their help, it was mildly annoying, almost as if they were saying, 'You are incapable of dealing with this on your own'. I had been taught to 'sort out my problems'.

And there were some instances, which I honestly was able to easily address and do exactly that. But I sat back one day, during the very early stages of the murder trial and thought about this.

I tried to think about it from the other persons perspective. I suddenly realised I wasn't being helpful for them, that I wasn't thinking about *their* needs. In other words, the moment I accepted their help, was the moment they felt as if they were contributing, making a difference, doing something, anything, to help.

By accepting, I was helping them along that path of usefulness and generosity. We all at times want to feel useful, and we will move mountains to show someone that we care enough about them or a situation to do this. And the great thing about this is it does help the person offering in many ways.

So, I started accepting. Whether it be material or spiritual, and not only from close relatives and friends but from strangers. That was the best thing I ever did, because now I felt better and at the same time, they did as well. To have a purpose can be so important.

Something else happened that had a huge positive impact on me in the early days. Because what happened to Jacquie was very high profile (It was the lead news story on News at Ten, The BBC, national and local TV and headlined the countries leading tabloids and appeared in true life magazines) It was even popping up in news reports all around the world.

I started getting sackfuls of goodwill and sympathy cards. There was even a card from a middle-aged woman, who lived in Australia, and who used to go dog walking along a river every day with her husband, the contents of the card were beautiful.

Messages of hope and help continued to arrive, then one day I sat down to think about all this. First of all, I was over-whelmed. These were absolute strangers, but I felt this connection with each one of them. It was like dropping a stone in a pond and watching the ripples spread out in circles, it seemed to be touching everyone. But more importantly, it was proof to me that there are lots of thoughtful, kind, compassionate people out there, not just in the UK, but all around the world, that even though they didn't know me or the boys, wanted to do something, anything to help. The fact that they put pen to paper to illustrate their kind support was gratefully received by me, and helped me so much emotionally at that time.

I did my best to reply to many of them, but if you happen to be one of those many people, that are now reading this book, and you wrote to offer a kind word. Please, may I say, thank you so very much! It helped myself, Aidan, Ben and Oliver, set off on our journey, and get to where we are today.

Epilogue

At the time of writing this, almost thirteen years have passed since Jacquie was murdered. So where are we all now, when so much time has passed? How have we all coped? How have we turned out? How well adjusted and happy are we?

AIDAN

He is now 31 years old. He's a lovely Guy, great sense of humour, a successful filmmaker, Director and Videographer. He also lives in Manchester and in a serious relationship, and besides work, has a wonderful, amazing set of friends, and his world is filled with music (we have a talented musician here) and laughter.

BEN

Is 20 years of age. Very independent, and an accomplished personal trainer and gym instructor, to the extent that he has now moved into being self-employed as a personal trainer. And quite rightly so, he knows his stuff, and all those years when he was much younger, working in one of my hairdressing salons as receptionist/shampooist etc. taught him his social and communication skills, which has stood him in good stead in his new self-employment.

He shares a house with two other friends half an hour away from us and loves every minute of it, but still regularly comes back to see us.

OLIVER

He is 17. A talented tennis player, he has an aptitude for photography. He has the keenest of creative eyes, which led him naturally to embark on an online diploma photography course (three modules down with very high marks in each) but is currently seeking work and training as a photographic apprentice with a reputable, established professional photographer.

And, on his own bat, without any help from me, he has managed to grab himself a part-time job in a local fish and chip shop, to earn a little spending money.

I am enormously proud of each one of them and considering what they have been through; they are as well adjusted and happy as I could expect of anyone.

Their success is not all down to me of course, sure, I have been there to help, to love, to guide, to point in the right direction, but they have come out on the other side with the right attitude, being honest and helpful, and sociably easy to fit into any situation.

So I pat my self on the back when I have time to stand back and take it all in, and I can be heard to mutter occasionally "I must have been doing something right!"

And me? Well, when it all happened in 2005, I had a number of Hair and Beauty salons, a full-time self-employed Hairdresser, but in the midst of all this, with everything else I was having to deal with, I decided to change jobs drastically!

I have always been sporty, competed in Athletics for my country, a ski instructor, Midland counties hockey player and a 2nd Dan Martial Artist. But the Hairdressing businesses gave me the freedom to pursue my other passions, which were acting and modelling.

But I realised I wanted to become more involved in a sport.

Moved out and sold up everything to do with Hair and Beauty, and started to develop a fitness brand, a class I called KETTFusion (a mixture of kettlebells and martial arts exercises) this all started in 2013, and now, it is an award-winning fitness brand, not only here in the UK, but in three other European countries, and have KETTFusion instructors qualifying all the time.

To say I kept myself busy during everything that happened to Jacquie and beyond is probably an understatement, but it was also my saving grace. I couldn't imagine, sitting at home on the sofa twiddling my thumbs all day, I would have gone stark raving mad!

So, here we are, I believe Jacquie would be proud of me, and especially the boys, and in my mind, this was the culmination of all my hopes and goals.

If there is one aspect of all this, which I hope you, the reader, can appreciate, is that everything and anything are possible, and that everything moves on. Moving on isn't so much the problem, because, as I mentioned in an earlier chapter, in my mind there is proof of this, what can be difficult is finding the energy to get up, reaching for that first hand-hold, that first step, and that can be harder than hell, but I promise you, the moment you make that first move, you have started on that journey.

That doesn't mean it will be plain sailing. It will end up being an interesting journey, a little like travelling on a train, where you will stop at various stations, to experience and wonder and take on board, but that train will be off again. You are the engine and conductor, not always sure where the next station is, but being able to rest assured the train will not stop there for ever.

There will always be a place for experts in all the relevant fields that may be associated with tragedy's like this, that can affect us, but always remember, empathy from those that have been in similar situations is invaluable, particularly from the aspect that it can feel comforting to know that you are not the only person in the whole wide world that something like this has happened to.

Organisations like WAY (Widowed and Young), Grief Encounter, Winstons Wish and Child Bereavement UK for example, can offer tremendous help, at a time when all you need is a helping hand and the emotional security, to help suggest ways of setting you off on your train journey.

Finally, I have a lovely friend, of similar background, who was having a difficult time adapting and moving on. One day she asked me, "You are a very close friend to me, and I know I can wholeheartedly rely on you to help me, thank you." I replied, "Yes, and I will always be here, but I am not that sort of friend who will stand with you high up on that cliff edge, holding your hand as you jump over the edge if everything is becoming difficult to cope with. I am that friend, who will be waiting at the bottom to catch you, just in case you fall!".

Many years ago, when Jacquie was alive, I was invited along to go to a local poetry society evening, to listen to an exciting new poet called Tariq Latif. I have to point out that until that point, I could take or leave poetry, so to say I wasn't overjoyed to hear Tariq read his poems that night, was an understatement. However, the first of his poems he read out, completely changed my perception of poetry.

The poem he read out was called 'Tell Her'. What was particularly interesting, was that Tariq explained in detail the inspiration for composing the poem. A personal story, which revolved around him seeing a girl at college that he desperately wanted to meet, but was too shy to ask her out on a date. However, he managed to get her home telephone number, and many times was trying to build up the courage to speak to her, but at the last minute put the phone down. After several attempts, he finally let it ring and waited for it to be answered, but it was her boyfriend!. "Yes? who's calling?" said the boyfriend. "My name is Tariq, a friend from college, please could I speak to …?".

"I'm afraid she is out at the moment", said the boyfriend, "But if you want to leave a message, I will pass it on to her?". And so we come to the title of the poem, 'Tell Her'.

This story mirrored in many ways how Jacquie and I met, and because of it, we both loved this poem so much, how it seemed to say everything I wanted to say to Jacquie, and what she wanted to say to me. And so, with kind permission from Tariq himself, here is an abridged version of that beautiful poem, taken from his book of poems, 'The Minister's Garden'. (Arc Publications).

Tell Her by Tariq Latif.

that one poem follows another

that two seeds yield a forest

that ice, water and steam are the same

that none of the four elements are elements

that our fifth finger evolved into a thumb

that breath connects us to all life

that each breath makes up a moment

that each moment is different

that I do what I can for us and them

that there are more than ten ways of saying

I love you

Dedicated organisations that provide
child bereavement services, and offers help
and advice for widows and
widowers with, or without children.

GRIEF ENCOUNTER

The Lodge, 17 East End Road, London N3 3QE

contact@griefencounter.org.uk

www.griefencounter.org.uk

Tel: 020 8371 8455

WAY (Widowed and Young)

Suite 17, College Business Centre, Uttoxeter Road, Derby

DE22 3WZ

enquiries@widowedandyoung.org.uk

www.widowedandyoung.org.uk

NB. There is a dedicated helpline number
available for members only.

PTO

CHILD BEREAVEMENT UK

Supports families and educates professionals when a baby

or child of any age dies or is facing bereavement.

Helpline: 0800 02 888 40

Email: support@childbereavementuk.org

Website: www.childbereavementuk.org

A Special Song, Played At The Memorial Service, Composed and Produced by Aidan Belizaire, My Eldest Son.

Sunshine in the morning and I'm fine.

I'm happy to be alive.

My sky is blue all the time.

Dive into the deep end of life's luxuries,

The one's that don't cost money.

Because life isn't a form of currency.

If you have everything you want,

Do you ask for more?

If you need cash quick, would you steal it?

Would you break the law?

To get what you want, what you don't really need

You ignore all the things that come for free

And these are the best things in your life

Children playing, laughing, smiling.

Well these all come for free

And a child's life should hold no misery.

Helping a blind man across the road today.

He repays you with a smile that warms you from the inside,

On a cold day and I know I'm ok

To get what you want

What you don't really need

No one can take that away from me

You ignore all the things that come for free

And these are the best things in your

Cause I've got what I want

What I do really need

No one can take that away from me

Don't ignore all the things that come for free

'Cause these are the best things in your

'Cause these are the best things in your

'Cause these are the best things in your

'Cause these are the best things in your life.

The Author: Michael Ross

I feel all of us have different 'skill' sets. I take a lot of pleasure out of helping others, I have always done that and will continue to do so.

I have had a few people say to me, "Well my partner died and left me with children, but he (or she) died of natural causes, nothing as terrible as the manner in which your wife died".

I immediately stress, that it doesn't really matter how someone died, the loss of a loved one can be devastating and upsetting, no matter what the circumstances were, but luckily help is at hand and all you have to do is reach out for it.

I now try to live life to the full, make the most of each day, and have come to terms with the fact that on the one hand, as human beings, we can be so very resilient, but on the other hand, our precious lives may be snuffed out in a fraction of a second. I have a motto, and that motto is:

'We are all friends, but I simply haven't met you all yet!'

Take care,

Michael.

Demon Beauty

A beauty and the beast retelling

Stefanie Simpson

We're all monsters here.

Acknowledgements

Thank you to everyone who's helped and supported me through writing this. The Witling Writers, as ever, my critique group, and all the Writers of Twitter, helping me procrastinate every day. I'd also like to thank everyone who's read Demon Beauty on Wattpad.

War Comes

Rosalin woke up to a ringing bell. Panic filled her bones. Everyone knew what the bell meant. Attack.

Rosalin whipped out of her bed and into the bedroom, shivering as she shoved her long dark hair back. War raged in the south and now came for them.

Her father, wiry and pale, still in his nightshirt, shuffled out of his room. He clutched a candle in his shaking hand. Rosalin pulled on her work dress and boots and hurried out into the farmyard with her father calling after her to wait as he followed.

In the distance across the fields, were lights from the village. The peal of the bell echoed into the surrounding dark. There were no defences, just the bell's alarm. She despised the sound of it. Her heart thudded, and throat closed. They'd waited for the mighty southern state of Merevia to attack for so long, and now they'd come.

Rosalin's father peered over her shoulder, his poor eyesight seeing nothing in the dark. "What is it, can you see?" He trembled and sounded bewildered.

"They're not coming from the east or the road. They're approaching from the west."

"What do we do?" He scratched at his white beard.

"Do? Father, there is nothing we can do but wait. If they've come this far north we..." Rosalin's dark eyes widened, her face contorted as flames ignited, the frightened cries of people joined the ringing of the bell, and then it stilled.

The horrified sounds of the villagers rose in the breeze as it carried the first whispers of smoke. Rosalin's father clutched his child. This was it.

Bands of soldiers and the horrors they unleashed on the small northern counties were upon them.

"Father, you should get ready to leave. The soldiers will be here soon, and we should be gone." Rosalin's flat tone belied her panic and pushed it down as she had for the past five years.

She turned away, going back inside to prepare for the journey. The farm was her whole life, comfortable but shabby, though the war had taken its toll. Once full of life and comfort, joy had been taken with the grinding weariness of scarce provisions, no trade markets, and grief from a relentless war fought over land. She readied saddlebags of winter provisions, only thinking of survival; it's all she had left. With a plan forming, she changed into trousers for riding as they bundled up for the cold and saddled their two horses.

For a moment, a pang of longing for the once loving, happy life she knew took her breath. The picturesque countryside and dull but lively village were ravaged and desolate.

Before the war, the farm-rich land of the northern counties had traded with the south and west coast for years, but a new regime came and gobbled up farms and towns, taking all as they crawled up the fishing ports, fighting battle after battle on the way. Her brothers died. Her mother died from her grief. A village of old people and children remained. Rosalin should be married, have her own family, but there was no one to care for her father, and she'd been left to run the farm alone with no prospects. She was tall,

had a good figure, and was healthy and lively, which would have counted for much in the past, but meant nothing now. Rosalin huffed in bitterness as she mounted her horse.

That was her once, but no more. All the lost possibilities of her life made Rosalin go cold. Who could defend them, the old men and washerwomen?

Her father's face filled with fear as they rode out from the narrow and little used paths they took and into the dark pines that loomed beyond. Entering the vast East Gelthan Forest on a bitterly cold night was their only choice. Rosalin's face was blank.

Rosalin shuffled silently and huddled deeper into her cloak. She doubted this was what her father had in mind when he'd taught her to hunt when she was younger.

At least those skills came in useful in the forests; men and animals weren't that different.

Her clothes were thick and stiff with filth, her skin dirty and figure wasted. Rosalin had hacked off her long, annoying braid weeks ago, and her short hair sat tucked behind her ears.

She'd lost all sense of time and place in the forest, but the winter wore on, and it was emptying out of the bandits and folk fleeing the war. There was less to scavenge, and less to fight for. It was always hunt or be hunted, and Rosalin never lost.

Two men, southern enemy soldiers in front of a meagre fire, argued loud enough for her to track them for a mile.

Sneering and salivating at the scent of food and heat, she waited like a patient predator as she focused on her prey.

"It's not true." The larger soldier shifted.

"It is – they killed him and put his head on a pike," the smaller and younger one said.

"I was there, and they didn't."

She neared in a half-crouch, invisible in the dark, and braced to attack.

"Henson put the dagger to his throat, and then cut his head off. There was so much blood that he slipped right over in it."

"I was with Henson, and that didn't happen." The bigger one threw another log on the fire, making it hiss and smoke.

Rosalin drew her own dagger, quietly moved forward, making no noise as she took a slow breath in, and reached over to take both the soldier's short sword and stab him in the side where the armour parted.

The second soldier barely saw her but drew his blade at the gurgle and splutter of his compatriot.

With the short sword in one hand and the bloody dagger in the other, she ducked and lunged at the soldier, little more than a child, and ran him through in a heartbeat.

In a moment of stillness, she allowed the fire to warm her, not looking at the bodies. The fire in her dead, wide eyes and shadows on her gaunt face danced in the warm light.

They weren't the first she'd killed and wouldn't be the last. It had to have been more than four months of bitter cold in the dark woods, and the smallest fire was a balm, even after killing two men. She knew, had it been the other way around, they'd have done the same – or worse.

She and her father had seen more than one body hanging from a tree, mutilated beyond recognition.

Absently rifling through the soldiers' things, she lamented there were no horses as their own had died and found little of use.

Rosalin kicked out the fire.

Taking what food and drink there was, as well as their weapons, she headed back to her father. The cold seeped back into her bones as she moved away from the residual heat. Rosalin didn't give the soldiers another thought as she returned to her camp. It was the reality of a long war, and everyone lived it. Everyone died in the end. It was a matter of when.

"Father."

The man, shrunken and shrivelled, appeared to have aged ten years as he stared at the remnants of their own fire.

She briefly remembered the image of him when he was younger. He laughed in warm summer sun as she chased a chicken in the yard. Her mother shelled peas, singing, and her brothers brushed down the horses, teasing their little sister.

She tucked the memory away again and relit the fire as they ate what they had left.

"Where did you get this?"

"Two soldiers on the road."

"It was good of them to share it."

Rosalin didn't say they were the enemy. She didn't say anything at all. The unspoken truth lay between them.

Rosalin watched her father sleep. He'd die soon. Those words went through her head, but she didn't feel any sorrow. It would be easier to travel, but he was the last thread left. He held her to the past.

Her own eyes barely closed. Exhaustion was something she was and rest an alien thought.

In the dim light of morning she spoke, "We can't stay here much longer, we have to chance it or starve."

Her father said nothing. Months of fearing the road, they'd stayed in the cover of the east woods all winter, but it had been too long, and Rosalin needed news of the war.

A day's walk led them out to open ground. Before them lay farm country. The air was warmer, and in the distance, mountains rose. To the west, forests rolled over hills, and they saw nothing but countryside.

Her father turned all about. "I don't know where we are. All the forest and the roads, with no sun to see, no horizon. I've only known flatlands. As long as we haven't veered to the West Gelthan Woods, I think we'll be fine." He wheezed a breath. "I was never one for maps."

Rosalin murmured, "Mother was the one for maps." She set her hood back. "I think we have passed back north, but to the east. If we carry on, I think we might reach the cattle scrubs and the wool market if it's still there. Not that far from home."

Before her father could reply, she walked on, and the sun on her face was a sweetness she never thought she'd know again.

By the next day they were out of provisions, and Rosalin went hunting rabbits in the scrubby brush and hedges at the bottom of the hill. She crouched and waited after spotting a burrow, dagger in hand. With quick, deft movements, she caught two, dispatching them quickly. With them tied and hanging over her shoulder, she went back to her father.

He was asleep.

"I have rabbits, father, can you help me prepare them?" She lit a fire. "Father?"

She looked up at where he was propped against a tree and blinked. He didn't move, his chest no longer rose and fell, and his skin was already grey.

Rosalin didn't even check his pulse. She didn't cry, couldn't, but hung her head and took a deep breath. He needed to be buried. Under the tree was as good a place as any to put him. Using the short sword, she dug a hole, and it took so long that the sunset by the time it was deep and big enough. Sweat covered her, panting into the night as she sat on the edge of the grave before throwing the blunted and battered sword.

6

Peering out into the darkness, the stars lit the moonless sky, and she wondered what she should do. She shivered as her body steamed in the cold. There was nothing else to do but go on. There was no going back. She gritted her teeth as she remembered the smell of her mother's bread and the large cosy hearth where her oldest brother would read to them at night. Weariness took over at the stories her mother wove came to mind. Tales of the magical west wood and the sound of her soft lyrical voice before bed with them all gathered at the hearth.

Her heart hurt, and resolve cracked.

Rosalin steadied her breath, opening and closed her fists, and hissed at the blistered skin on her palms.

Taking the last of the water, she stood and heaved her father's body into the grave with a cry, covered him over with her hands, hauling the mounds of soil, hovering between numb pain and fury, and patted the earth down when she was done. She stood for few minutes, swaying. The wind rose, bringing colder air, but she ignored it. Looking down at the ground where he'd spend eternity, she remembered him as he was and let that pain come.

Her father could sing. Long bawdy songs that her mother would chastise him for. A bubble of laughter rose up that turned into a single strange sob.

Rosalin tipped her head back to the stars and cursed whatever fates or gods wrought war upon simple people who just wanted to live. They killed laughter and song and everything beautiful and ordinary. She missed being ordinary.

Turning from her father's grave, she pulled on her cloak and picked up her gear, taking the rabbits with her and went into the night. She made her way downhill, across farmland and fallow ground and found a neglected road.

She thought heading northeast to the empty scrublands where small cattle farms were, there would be fewer signs of war, but the neglected road

deteriorated. When far away enough from her father's death to stop, she made camp.

Perhaps she'd gone in the wrong direction. Maybe the sheep farmers were long gone, and the wool market closed.

She made a fire to ward off the bitter dark and cold in a small clearing off the road and skinned and gutted one of the rabbits. She wasn't hungry but needed to eat – even if preparing the animal made her feel sick.

In the quiet of the fire crackling and smell and smoke of roasting meat, she let her body relax. Was it a terrible thing to be a little relieved her father was gone? She no longer had to share awkward silence with him; it was hers alone. Sometimes pain was better dealt with alone. No eyes on her to see or to worry.

Rosalin ate all the meat, her bony fingers thick with grease, but she didn't care. She closed her eyes for a moment, close to the fire. Wrapped up in her thick cloak, and with a full belly, she hunkered down for a sleepless night, fending off the dark and horror.

Motives

Sitting up in the dark with sweat prickling, her skin chilled. The fire had gone out, and she shivered. The lumpy ground dug in, and her back was numb as she got up. The dull, creeping sun urged her to pack up and head onward. As she walked, all she wanted was a bath and a bed. This life had become so normal and she wondered if she could go back to living that way. A house with dull everyday chores. Friends. She brushed it off. Paramount was finding a safe road and avoiding anyone in a soldier's uniform.

The day wore on, and air warmed, the road worsened as it veered back south, and by what must have been noon, she halted as deep muddy ruts filled the way. Rosalin studied the cloud and felt rain in the air.

Scrubbing her face, she considered changing direction, maybe west, but that meant heading into the West Gelthan Forest if she wanted to stay off the road. Rosalin shuddered. She and her father avoided it at all costs. There were stories of whole platoons going into it and never been seen again. The evil that dwelt there was no joke. Her mother told her that.

Then she heard it. The distant sound of marching, and under it the rumble of carts.

Rosalin darted into the trees, rushing as far from the sound as she could. The light patter of rain hit her as she fled.

She'd heard – and seen – what happened to women and children at the hands of the armies, and though she was proficient enough at taking care of herself, a whole infantry was beyond her skills.

The wet mulch became boggy underfoot as she fled further away from the road, but she took no heed. She only heard her heart beating and the harsh sound of her breath burning in and out of her lungs. Turning a little behind her, she misstepped, and tumbled down an incline, her pack slamming into her, and promptly knocked herself out.

Rosalin tasted the lingering tang of bile and groaned. Her stomach complained, and she tried to sit up but couldn't. Waist deep in sticky mud, her heavy pack pulled her down, and the remaining rabbit was missing.

Unable to move her feet, she struggled from her top half, trying to wriggle free of the straps. She wrenched an arm out and reached for a tree root, her fingers straining for it.

"Well, well, lads, look what I found," the very male voice called in an amused tone.

Rosalin froze. Her eyes slowly travelled up the incline, and a soldier looked over the ridge.

"Saw your tracks, thought to myself, look at that, looks like someone fleeing. Thought you were a deserter. Not by the look of you, eh?"

She didn't reply.

"Want a hand?"

"For what reason? To be raped or sold as a slave?"

The amusement on his face vanished. "I can assure you that no harm will come to you. Northern?"

She gave him a hard look, and understanding registered between them. With a nod, he scrambled down the drop, and reaching for her hand, pulled

her out. She came out with a slurp and pop. Her body plastered with freezing mud, and she shook.

Handsome and fair with a strong jaw and nose, and an officer by the look of him.

Rosalin turned to pull out her pack, but it was gone. It was all she had left in the world other than for her concealed purse and weapons. At least she still had them.

"How long have you been on the road?"

She turned back to him, her mouth set in a line. "I don't even know anymore. Less than half a year."

"I'd say from the northwest by your accent."

"Yes." Rosalin weighed her options, trying not to panic.

"Heard much news of the war?"

"No."

He took a breath. "Everything was burnt. People are migrating back, resettling or rebuilding. You could go back." His curious eyes set her teeth on edge.

"Everyone's dead." She frowned and shook her numb arms.

"Where are you going then?"

Wiping the excess mud from her, she cleared her throat.

"You don't know, do you?"

"No. We fled."

"Where are your companions?"

"Dead," Rosalin snapped.

After a moment of silence, he spoke. "We're heading home, but it's a long journey. Merveis City is three weeks march. There are some refugees and stragglers at the back. The war is over."

"For you. Do I have a choice?"

"Of course. You can do as you please. But it's not safe here."

"Nowhere's safe anymore. Safe doesn't exist unless you're the victor, and that's not me."

"Captain Henson, what you doing?" a gruff bawdy voice called out, and the man in front of her rolled his eyes.

"Rescuing a damsel in distress." The captain grinned at her; it was far too wide and charming. Rosalin didn't like it.

"Well, we have food at least. Come. You won't be hurt."

Closing her eyes for a moment, she reigned in her impulse to stab him, and focused on the fading light instead, Rosalin was nothing if not pragmatic. She might as well eat. "Fine."

The captain helped her as they climbed the hill.

"Do you have a name?"

"Rosalin."

She walked down the lines of soldiers making camp with their eyes on her.

The captain left her with a group of overly dressed and painted people; among them women and delicate youths, men of all shapes and sizes, and those who bore no gender. Rosalin missed the bright joy of life and the variance of the people of home.

Rosalin stood awkwardly at the fringe, and an older woman in a blue dress, to whom the others deferred, brought her into their circle.

"Oh dear, what happened to you?"

Rosalin didn't answer, and the woman's smile fell away.

"We can clean you up, find you some clothes."

"Thank you."

Behind the cart the group rode on, someone put a half barrel filled with water. Keeping her eyes on camp as she crouched and undressed, she slipped her weapons into the underside of the cart, wedging them in.

Rosalin washed in the cold water and using a slither of plain soap; it was the closest she'd been to being clean in months.

A youth put a fresh set of clothes nearby – a simple tunic and leather trousers – and once dressed, she cleaned up her boots, and washed her clothes in the dirty wash water, leaving them on the wagon to dry, and tucked her purse into her trousers. Someone handed her a snug leather jacket, and it warmed her chilled skin as she ran her fingers through her wet hair by the fire.

The woman in the blue dress watched Rosalin and handed her a delicious tea and hard flatbread with meat and dried fruit when Rosalin finished. It was a feast.

"Better?" the woman asked.

Rosalin sighed in relief, and the tea reminded her of home as she sipped it. "Much."

"I'm Callie, are you heading to Merveis?" The woman eyed Rosalin as they ate.

"Perhaps. I've never been to a city. I just want to be somewhere safe."

"It's not particularly safe. What do you want?"

"I don't know. I've nowhere to go. How are you all this far north?"

"We are with the soldiers, we travel behind, gather up those willing to be with us, and carry them away. We stick together under the protection of the guard. It's the nature of war, dear. Still, all over with now, time to go home. Be that what you make of it, for home can change." The woman's refined face looked almost dangerous in the firelight, and the hair on the back of Rosalin's neck prickled.

The companions settled around their fire, drinking and talking, and later, a few of them headed up into the ranks.

Next to Rosalin sat a slim youth with slight hands, working a willow basket in the firelight. They worked deftly and chatted happily with the others.

She became tired, and her eyes nodded as she watched the rhythmic movements of their hands. The youth hummed a tune, and Rosalin leant back and went to sleep, taking rest while she could.

Without the responsibility of her father, she let something of the past go. Her dreams were disturbed and woke several times, and the last time, she couldn't get back to sleep.

Getting up, she walked around the camp, dawn already in the air.

"You shouldn't stray." The captain appeared out of the dark, his armour and cloak shone in the moonlight.

"I'm not used to people. What are you doing this end of the caravan?"

"Perimeter checks." The other soldiers wandered past. "People will rise soon and make their way. It's a long day's march."

She didn't want to go. Couldn't. Something held her back. She glanced over at the people beginning to rise; the light hum of sleepy activity and the start of a hard day.

Henson straightened his shoulders. "You're not coming."

"I have nothing, and it's logical. I don't want to travel to a city full of the people who killed my family and everyone I knew."

"I understand." His face tensed. "But I can't let you go."

"You said I was free to." He was handsome, strong, capable and charming, but something else lurked behind those eyes. Henson. It only occurred to her then, she'd forgotten about the two soldiers. Whose head had he cut off?

He smiled at her. "It's not safe."

"Nor am I."

His look changed, eyes raking over her. Rosalin closed hers, blocking him out.

"You'll come. You have nothing."

That wasn't entirely true. Rosalin could take some provisions from the food store, a flask, her other clothes, and the small bag of coin tucked away in her trousers. Along with her dagger and the short sword she'd hidden.

Someone called the captain, and he stepped away reluctantly, speaking to the older woman. Rosalin crept back to the cart, watching the sluggish movement of the camp. Ducking low, she gathered her things, setting the blunt sword at her back under her old cloak, took food from the supply barrels while Callie's back was turned, and slipped out into the forest that enclosed the road. She bundled her old clothes and food up, tying it to her front as she went. It would be hard without her cooking gear, napkins, and tools, but at least she had a few things. She'd adapt, she always did.

Instead of the road, she headed west into the forest, not knowing where she would end up. Tales of horror and fear were vivid as she moved through the trees. Magic in the hills of the West Galthen Forest encroached. Old women passed those tales down to children for generations, and it was hard not to be afraid.

People were wary of it, and no one crossed onto that side. Even Rosalin and her father skirted it until they reached the Galthen road through the forest that cut it in two. They headed straight into the danger of the East Forest without thought. It was odd as she thought about it, so much superstition, yet other than in tales, there wasn't any proof. Rosalin was too desperate to care. Besides, the southerners didn't want to venture into it.

The ground was drier and steep, and she barely made tracks. Rosalin marched with what energy she had across the wooded land. She heard no one follow, and she made time. The food from the evening giving her a push of strength.

Her cloak was still damp and dirty, but it was cover enough for the day. The trees bore the first signs of spring, though it was still winter, and pines changed into oaks and birch. Ferns coiled underfoot, and she heard a few birds as she went deeper in.

Reaching a steep peak that opened into a clearing, she saw the landscape beyond. For as far as she could see lay hill and wood. No towns or cities in sight. She was both relieved and afraid. It was beautiful and green. Too green. The east forest had been dark and bare from winter. With a frown she sat, staring out, and ate a chunk of flatbread and meat, relishing the feel of the sun and a sweet breeze. Rosalin needed a plan. Get through the woods, perhaps to the coast. She could go to sea. Not that she'd ever seen the water. She looked behind her, and what awaited her if she went back, and with a sigh, she headed into the lush unknown, her path chosen, and whatever fate lay ahead.

Hours later, with her legs aching, she passed through a valley with a pretty stream and drank deep, filling the canteen. The water was pure and crisp. She'd not tasted anything so wonderful for years. Ahead of her was a small path, little used. She wandered it cautiously, and seeing a familiar bush laden with ripe fruit, she took a handful of berries and ate them. She groaned at their sweet taste and the memories that followed. Her mother used to make them into wine. Rosalin remembered crushing them, and the days of work that she never got to taste. Rosalin licked the juice from her lips with the creeping feeling that something was wrong. It was the wrong time of year for them. She dropped the last of the berries, and her curiosity got the better of her.

Her mother always called her an inquisitive child, wanting to know everything, and it always led to trouble.

She followed as the bushes thickened and over grew, and she pushed through them until it opened out into a garden.

Rosalin looked about in wonder. The earth was dark and rich, neatly cultivated into beds, fruit and vegetables grew amongst lavender and leafy vines as if in late summer, ready to harvest.

A hedged square enclosed the large maze of beds, and she moved along the central path as it broke into a formal garden. Out of nowhere, it seemed, loomed a tall building.

She hadn't seen that from the hill. She gawped at the pale, yellow stone tower, and the castle attached to it.

Where had this come from?

Turning in a circle, a fox ambled passed her feet. A crow cawed. The fox sat to her left and watched her, and the crow flew down, perching nearby.

She walked past them, and they watched her go. Perhaps she hit her head too hard yesterday or maybe there was something wrong with the berries she just ate.

The building was old and cracked with signs of age. The ornate stone front steps were no less impressive for the weeds that covered them.

It looked abandoned. It wasn't; no garden would look like that without constant care.

Rosalin had few choices, and she needed food. Maybe a bath. Hopefully, the people who lived there might need help or could spare her some charity. Weariness outweighed all else; fear and death had changed her, but in that garden and sun, she wanted more. There was hope.

With a shrug, Rosalin made the steps and knocked the large tarnished brass knocker. The sound rang out. Nothing. She knocked again. Maybe it was abandoned.

Sighing, she sat down, drinking some of the water. The fox padded up to her and sat at the bottom of the steps. Rosalin felt odd, watched. She turned and looked back, scanning the many windows, and saw nothing. She turned back to the patient little fox.

"My father used to hunt you for getting to our chickens. Always made me sad, but I liked eggs more."

She pulled out the last of her bread and tore the creature off a chunk and threw it down to him. The thing scarfed it down.

Rosalin rested before wandering around the outside of the building and found the kitchen doors down a flight of steps that lead into a paved courtyard with washing lines, and herbs lined the edges, scenting the air. She peered through the leaded window and knocked the door. Hearing something behind her, she found the fox.

"I've made a friend, huh?" She gave him a loping smile and turned back to the door. The fox jumped up and scratched at the wood.

Rosalin frowned and tried the handle. Finding it unlocked, she opened the door and poked her head through a narrow gap. The kitchen was huge but felt unused and the air stale.

"Hello?" Her voice echoed off stone as she edged inside.

The castle was dark and fires cold as if everyone had gone away leaving it for the next occupant. She ran her finger in the light dust that covered the large table, hesitating for a minute. Then she huffed at herself; there was no one there, so who cared if she sought shelter. She walked through the kitchen and upstairs to the main house.

Rosalin noticed scarce furniture, no comforts, no candles in the sconces and lamps sat unlit; there was nothing much of anything, except empty rooms. There were a lot of those, the main one of which was a cavernous empty hall. Several large rooms sat off it, all sparsely furnished.

The fox followed the whole time. "You're allowed in the house?" The fox just looked at her. "Hello!" Nothing. No sounds, no stirring, only a jarring solitude. "Where is everyone?"

She found a small room, near the stairs to the kitchen, and it felt almost cosy. The hearth had a fire laid with a comfortable chair, and stacks of old books. Along one wall, dozens of scrolls and volumes were neatly set out over long narrow draws. Picking up one of the richly bound books, she couldn't make out any of the words, and it smelt musty. The day cooled, and she was tired. At least it was mostly dry and comfortable in that room.

Rosalin debated what to do, but the hearth called to her. It was too tempting not to.

She lit the fire, finding the wood dry and sweet-scented like applewood, she put the bundle of her things she'd tied to her front down, along with the sword, and sat on the chair by the fire as it took. It was nice to be by a fireplace again. She stared into the flames thinking of her father, swallowing back the sight of his grey body. Her mind wandered to the soldiers she'd cut down, and what they said about Henson.

Rosalin thought of the day her brothers went off to war.

She thought of the person she became.

Finally, Rosalin went to sleep.

Master

Taking a deep breath, Rosalin knew she wasn't alone. Before she even opened her eyes, she felt a presence. Not the fox, but the air felt different. Heavier and hotter.

"I know you're awake."

Rosalin opened her eyes at the deep and distorted voice.

"I am Lord here, and you're in my chair."

She blinked several times as her eyes adjusted to the dark.

From the firelit gloom, something emerged from the shadowed wall; a tall figure, clothed and almost a person but not, and loomed over her.

The dark red pits of his eyes shone, and curled horns pointed out from a smooth head. The creature was dark blue, almost charcoal, and skin wound with bluer circled and geometric patterns. His face though caught her attention. Roughly hewn; he looked carved, like a statue made real.

She froze; no emotion or thought showed on her face at the thing in front of her. Her mother's tales at night by the fire came back to her again. Rosalin sat on her lap as she rocked, talking of witches made of magic, of what dwelt in the west forest, which took evil people away. It was real. She swallowed her shock and breathed again.

"You're lost, little girl."

"Girl? I haven't been one of those for a very long time," Rosalin murmured, not taking her eyes off it. She tensed, unable to grasp it, unaware that she'd spoken.

"Do I frighten you, girl?" He bared his white fangs.

"What are you?"

In the silence as the fire crackled the creature watched her, and she watched him. The only other sound was the fox snoring in front of the flames, who finally lifted his head, yawned, and sat up. The tension broke, and Rosalin blinked. The creature took up all the space, filling it with a hot presence, and the dark of the room closed in on her.

"What is this place?"

He grunted. "Magic and danger. And my home." He pushed off the wall, built the fire up, and patted the fox.

"Then I apologise. I did not mean to invade it. I knew someone must live here, but I couldn't find anyone." She spoke in a single quick breath, not feeling her legs.

"I know."

"You're being very reasonable."

The Lord snarled at her. She gripped the arms of the great big chair.

"I'm sorry." She got up and collected her things.

"What are you doing?"

"Leaving."

He pinned her with a stare, head tilted. "Stay. It is the middle of the night, stay one night, at least." He stretched out to his full height.

"Thank you." Her voice shook, and hand went to her waist.

"Don't bother with the dagger. It won't do anything. Come, eat with me." He turned and led the way. She followed, heart hammering in her chest.

He wore ancient breeches, and an open shirt; homespun by their look, yet his feet were bare and like hers. They moved through the dark castle, cold and damp, and she shivered.

They went in silence, only their feet making noise in the dim passages, her fear grew with each loud step, and her impulse to run increased with every moment in a delayed reaction. After a few minutes, disorientation in the dark made her dizzy. She put her hands out to feel the way but touched nothing. Sweat gathered on her skin. She followed closely, afraid to be lost.

The stairwell he led her to was pitch black as they went down. It was too much, and her footing faltered. "I can't see."

He stopped in front of her, she bumped into the solid and hot creature.

"I forgot. I do not keep the company of men."

"I'm not a man."

"I thought you said you were not a girl?"

"I'm a woman."

He laughed. A rasping sound. Suddenly there was light in the sconce nearby, and she blinked.

The fox was behind her and nudged her when the creature began to walk again. Curiosity overtook her shock. "What's your name, are you a man, you said you were Lord. Like, a lord? Or the Lord. Does that mean you're male-"

"My name is Crawt. I'm Lord of here. I suppose I am male. Gender as mortals view it, is not something we consider because we are all this." He gestured to himself, and turned, considering her question. "But I suppose we are male." He ran his lip over a fang and turned back, heading on.

The kitchen was transformed by bright light from lamps filled with a luminous liquid, and the room flickered and glowed. The stove threw out comforting heat, and on the table lay a wealth of fruit. It was welcoming. The fox curled up by the stove and went back to sleep.

Above the oven on a perch over the mantle, the crow flapped its wings, cawing as its head darted up and down, and little black eyes watched her. After a moment of noise, it settled down, tucking in its wings and snuggled in on itself.

Crawt's black horns and blue-grey skin shone in the ethereal light, and the delicate patterns that covered him were a more vivid blue in the brighter light. She took everything about him in, even the fangs that poked out.

He looked like every terrifying monster used to frighten children, and yet he bore an even stillness. He seemed calm and not evil. It was inexplicable. She should be terrified. Captain Henson made her more uncomfortable than whatever he was.

His manner was gentle as he gestured for her to sit. Taking the seat opposite, he regarded her, and she didn't know what to say or do. She waited. Would he eat her? Kill her? Do unspeakable things to her that her mother warned her of? Whatever his intent, it couldn't be any worse than what she'd seen, or done.

He tapped the table, his black nails clinking. "This land is hidden. Do you understand? It is forbidden to your kind. Yet, here you are." He spread his hands. "How? What magic did you use?"

"No magic. I found a stream and drank, saw some fruit, ate it, and here I am."

"You ate the fruit?"

Rosalin nodded.

"Hmm, here, you might as well eat more." His tone was severe as he scrutinised her.

She reached out for the fruit but wavered. "Are they magic?"

"Not dangerous magic." He leant forward, inspecting her face, eyes darting to the fruit. "Go on."

"What will happen?"

"You'll be fed, what a ridiculous question."

"Well, there's no need to be rude, you're a seven-foot..." Rosalin held the seat of the chair.

He spoke slowly, as if to a child. "Demon."

"Demon, I don't know what's in the fruit."

He laughed again with his head thrown back, and it echoed. He hummed in amusement. Picking a handful of berries, he ate them as he sat back. His mirth faded. "No one has found their way here in all the time I've dwelt in this place and lived. No single mortal has sat in my chair. How is it that you have?"

Rosalin made a little helpless gesture. "What will you do with me?"

"That is a good question. One I must think on. For now, eat your fill."

She ate. Part of her was afraid, but in the back of her mind, she wasn't truly alarmed. It was a shock, but not revulsion, not the fear she felt with Henson.

"Do you have a purpose?"

She shook her head.

"Why do you travel?"

"War. My home is gone."

He nodded slowly and rolled a berry in between his fingers. He popped it into his mouth, and then turned his head, going still. The patterns on his skin shimmered, and eyes grew hotter.

"I think you should stay here for a time until I figure you out. I swear you will come to no harm from my hand."

"Really?" She narrowed her eyes.

"You've wandered accidentally into my lands. There is magic here. It isn't good." He scraped his chair back, almost distracted.

Rosalin pocketed some of the fruit.

"You should rest."

Exasperating and strange, this creature bore magic and secrets, and she wanted to know everything. All thoughts of the grim months, of rabid survival, and her father's death faded when she was near him. "Who are you? At least tell me that."

"I was unmade and cursed and made a demon. I was also exiled," Crawt said, and his wry tone belied his blank face as he picked the torch up from

the sconce. "Leaving the underworld and arriving here was not easy, and I have power. Much of it spent. I am old now. Ancient in mortal terms. The world travels past me, and I do not see it. I no more take note of it than you do the life of that bird."

The crow cawed from its perch.

She didn't know what to say. After a few moments, she asked, "What are the crow and fox?"

"They are my companions. They come and go. They're just Crow and Fox."

His cryptic answers grated on her.

"Tomorrow, you will tell me your story. You will tell me everything I need to know."

Rosalin narrowed her eyes. "Am I a prisoner?"

He hesitated on the kitchen stairs. She held her makeshift pack tighter as he studied her face. The heat of the torch made her wince.

"No. But you cannot be left to wander. As I said, there is magic here, and I do not know why you are here."

She gave a firm nod, knowing there was little choice. Henson tried to keep her too, and her instinct told her to be wary, but though Rosalin was shocked, she was not itching to run. It was the opposite. He grunted and led the way through the great hall and up the grand staircase. She'd not explored that far.

From the damp gallery upstairs, he opened a door, showing her the room. "Here."

She found herself in a pretty and well-lit room. A large comfortable bed, good furniture, and even a rug.

She turned around.

"Is this acceptable?" he asked.

"It's more than I've ever known."

He grunted and left her after a pause.

With a slow breath, she sat on the bed. A wave of nausea in her stomach. Fox sat near the door. He licked his lips and cocked his head.

"Staying with me?"

He yawned and padded to the fire, curled up by it.

Rosalin found clothes and linens in the draws and cupboards, and through a door was a bathing room. At home, they'd had a tin bath they put in the yard, and here she had her own water pump.

A real bath was too good to pass up. Rosalin stuck a poker in the fire as her mother had done to heat water. She pumped and filled the ewer and filled the bath until half full. When the poker was hot, she wrapped her hand in a cloth, took the poker and shoved it in the bath, making the water hiss and steam.

It wasn't hot, but warm, and that was better than cold.

Slipping into the water, she dunked her head under, hoping to wash everything away, but some things could not be cleansed.

The water cooled, and she used the lavender and rose soap that was set out and scrubbed at her skin with a cloth.

Heaven was the simple joys after hardship, and no bath would ever feel that good again. Her pleasure was remote, far away. She watched it absently, appreciating it, but not feeling it as she once might have.

Climbing out, she wrapped herself in the coarse linen and squeezed her hair out. She stood looking at the murky water for a long time and the pattern of scum floating on the top.

Rosalin shook her head, and using the ewer to empty the water out, she sluiced it down the privy. Such a treat instead of squatting over hastily dug pits.

She wiped the bath out and went back into the bedroom. Fox snored by the fire. She went to the window and watched the wind rustle the trees. Relaxed on one hand, and ever restless on the other, she tried to be still, and let her thoughts take over.

Every mistake and evil deed she'd done to survive. Memories of peace, the blood on her hands, decisions she'd made, her father, all of it, pulsed in her thoughts. All abstract and yet painful. Rosalin shuddered a breath and brought herself to order.

Then she saw him. Hulking and unnerving, and it made her heart thump. He came out of the woods and looked up. She nearly winced and moved away but didn't; she watched him.

The moment passed, and he went inside.

What had she done?

"Tell me about your life," Crawt asked her.

He'd collected her from her room early and led her downstairs. They'd walked through the great hall – she could have stood in the fireplace the place was so big – and into the small room she'd found yesterday. Rosalin paid more attention. The rug was rich but worn to nothing. The fabrics faded, and stone walls looked dusty. The piles of books and scrolls were neat but numerous. Some were crumbling and others newer.

Rosalin sat on the small stool and he on the large chair.

She told him of the war and the toll it took.

"There is sea town in the west coastal region where both sides dug in, and my brothers were camped there. Mother was feeding the chickens when the news came. We couldn't bury them, but they brought their insignia. They fell together at least. Most of the men from our town died in that battle. She

fell to the floor in tears and barely spoke again. That winter when the sickness came, she died."

He frowned, leaning forward, intent on her. "And you and your father were left."

"We spent months in the east woods when our town was attacked. Deserters and other people fleeing the war were there too. Sometimes soldiers came in to clear us out. We avoided everyone that we could." Rosalin stared at a crack in the stone, and her foot nudged a frayed corner of the rug at the hearth.

Crawt shifted, and she looked at the ancient chair with thickly carved legs and faded cushion. Anything else was more interesting than her story, yet she found herself telling it.

"I'm very different to who I was. My mother would brush out my hair and braid it. It was so long. I miss that. I coveted nice dresses and fine fabrics. I wondered who I'd marry. I was happy in that life. When the war started, we never thought it'd come for us too, but life became harder. The trade markets closed, so no one had money. The men went to fight. Suddenly, my brothers were gone." Rosalin shivered, even for the warmth of the fire. "Watching mother die was the worst. Seeing father's spirit break... and then there was just me. I put away my pretty dresses and worked hard. Kept us going. Even in the woods." Tears filled her eyes, and she fought them back.

Rosalin couldn't examine the past, not yet, it was too painful. She held her breath, pressing down to quell the pain.

"A hard existence. Where would you go now?" he asked quietly.

Her eyes closed at his voice, easing out the breath, and let the tension go at his gentle tone. "The war is over, so I'm told. Maybe back north."

"Where north?"

"A small village just north of the market town of Toolin. Above the Ves river."

Crawt scowled with a nod. "You cannot go there from here it is too dangerous. Mountains to cross and magic to pass through. You'd have to go back and around. You'd have to take the roads."

Blinking off her mood, Rosalin was not that surprised after what he'd told her, and really, she didn't want to leave yet. Could she really stay with him? "Have you decided what to do with me?"

"I have been alone here too long. I cannot venture away. These lands are my sanctuary and prison." He glanced down at the fire with his mouth pulled down into a shrug.

The silence drew out. Rosalin stared at him, studying the markings on his skin again. They were jumbled at first glance, but the bluer markings were in several shapes and orders, circling other forms and cut with sharp lines. She wanted to read them like words. She frowned at the thought.

"You're a demon?" her voice trembled a little, desperate to know more. The reality in front of her was not hers, yet there it was, and couldn't be denied.

He smiled. "I am. I shall pick fruits from the garden for dinner."

Rosalin nearly laughed, then her stomach hurt and was dizzy again. "Do you have anything other than fruits? It's just I'm so hungry."

He nodded. "As you wish."

Gesturing for her to follow, she kept up, and his feet went quickly down through the rooms to the kitchen.

"Can you cook?"

"I can," Rosalin said, knowing what he would ask.

"Then see to your needs," Crawt scowled, looking about the kitchen. "I grind grain out of habit, I sometimes make bread, but not even fox will eat it. There is honey and salt."

Rosalin's eyebrows were in her hairline.

"Do you think because I am this that I do not need comfort? I must seek answers." He strolled out, and she watched his hulking frame disappear.

She huffed and sat as Fox came and nuzzled her.

There was no malice in Crawt. Surliness, but she didn't mind that.

She looked about the modestly stocked pantry, and no, it wasn't a cook's pantry, but there was enough to make a flatbread her mother would make when there was little left in winter. She sang a song absently as she baked, one her mother taught her, and quietly worked away. For a moment, she was Rosalin again, and the stillness grew on her. The sun streamed through the windows, and the quiet seeped into her mind. Such relief at that moment.

As the light failed, she sat by the stove while the flatbreads cooked.

Crawt joined her, she offered him the bread, and he gave her some fruit. They spread honey on the warm bread and made a modest meal of it.

"Why are you not afraid of me?" He focused on his food.

The words stuck in her throat, but she forced herself to say them. "I've seen things, killed people. I buried my father not long ago. It's possible I will be when my shock wears off."

His red eyes seared her. "I have thought about what to do with you. I wonder perhaps, would you wish to stay?"

"Why?"

He shifted, looking awkward. "I have been alone a long time. There is much work to do, and I never have time to do it all. The gardens and house. Perhaps you'd care to stay for a while. You have no plan or destination of need." Crawt attempted to look nonchalant. He didn't succeed.

Rosalin made her face still, so she didn't laugh. It was sweet. Could a demon be sweet? "Maybe I'll stay. I'll think about it."

"Good." A whisper of a smile played for a moment, making his fangs poke out, and he went back to his food.

Rosalin wondered if she shouldn't go to sea after all.

Horror

Crawt was nowhere to be found in the morning. She wandered the gardens, and the ever-present Fox and Crow followed her as she searched. She decided to stay. Shock or fear didn't come, and curiosity burnt in her about him and the magic around her. All thoughts of the sea were forgotten as his mystery consumed her.

Yet there was more to it than that, the unlooked-for peace and rest, and the sweet lull of a summer breeze and a bed were too inviting. Rosalin picked a sprig of a fragrant herb and breathed deep. The sweet scent caught the air, but the wind cooled.

Fox yawned and lay on the grass. She needed to know more about them too. The sky dulled, and rain threatened.

"Don't go that way."

She turned with a gasp. "You startled me."

"Apologies."

"It's fine, but not many can." Rosalin took a moment and watched him in the daylight, her cheeks burning in surprise. As he moved, the glittering patterns on his skin shimmered, and she kept blinking. Not quite believing it.

He pointed to the trees behind them. "You mustn't go that way."

"Why?"

"The magic I speak of is everywhere, it is the whole land. Look at me, do you suppose it to be good?"

"No, perhaps not but it doesn't feel malevolent here. Mother always said witches in the woods were evil."

Crawt pursed his lips in a smile. "I am not a witch, but anyone who wields power will fall to it eventually. Those woods, in the west, are full of things that should not be. They are contained. But they're not safe. Not for you."

"What would happen?"

"Depends on what you come across. It could be several things. I guard it as well as I can, but I am only one."

"If I stay," she said, turning and walking back to the gardens, "what do you want of me?"

"I thought you could help me. Equally, and perhaps eat together. I have books, and there are the gardens. It is not adventurous, and I am not much company."

"Can I leave if I chose?"

He hesitated. "You can leave whenever you wish. My only condition is that you stay out of these woods."

"That's fair. I'll stay, Crawt. Is that really your name?"

He gave her a flat look and went back into the woods, vanishing into the dark beyond the trees. She'd not even asked about Crow and Fox.

"Come on then." She said to no one as she walked back. Might as well set about going to work.

Rosalin explored every room again and found nothing but ancient dust and the decay of time. Had these rooms ever been really lived in? The castle felt cold and empty, unloved all but for a few rooms, ones Crawt used. The library was dark as the cloud rolled in, and rain pattered the window. Rosalin lit a lamp and set to studying what she could find. The books were so old,

she couldn't understand them, but the scrawl reminded her of the markings on Crawt's face alongside other languages.

Rosalin found maps. Drawers of them. She eagerly unrolled each one from its drawer. Some were of places she didn't recognise – whole continents that she didn't recognise – but one centred on the Gelthen forest. Divided into east and west by the road with all the lesser paths and ways that threaded and networked north to her home, the map showed her the stretch of wooded land that spread across her known world. Her country was divided by the great forest into north and south, and she studied where the main cities and towns were. It took a while to figure out which roads she had taken from the north west, across to the east, and into the trees. She'd been right, she and her father were way east and near the cattle scrubs. So close to home. Several days march full west, and they'd have been in Toolin.

There was little indication on the map where she was now, and she carefully rolled it up.

Another scroll, made of thick black fabric lay out, and her skin crawled. The markings were that of Crawt's body, and the same circled patterns covered it. Laid over it was the palace and all the grounds with it. The woods to the west were marked off and, in the centre, a white circle.

She swallowed her sudden fear, and hastily put it away as she shuddered her unease. Her hands shook, and she sat down. The day had worn away, and she tidied up.

Crawt appeared before dusk, and they ate together again.

"I'm going to get bored of fruit and bread." Rosalin dropped a berry onto her plate.

"Ah, some of the vegetables are nearly ready to pick."

"No meat?"

"I do not eat other creatures."

She blinked. "What about Fox and Crow?"

"Especially not them."

She laughed before taking a bite of bread. "I meant why do they follow me around."

He shook his head wryly. "Everything here, in time, becomes... enchanted. These two have followed me for a long time. I cannot remember if they were other things once."

"I don't understand." She put her bread down and sipped her water. "Are you enchanted? Will I become enchanted? What happened to you?"

"Do you always ask so many questions?" He ran his ran over his brow and slumped. "I keep the magic. It is my task. And I've not had any person here before, so I do not know. I am not enchanted, this is what I was made into long before your village was ever created. I have seen kingdoms fall and rise. I came here as punishment. I am still unrepentant and will remain here."

She opened her mouth to ask another question, but he held his hand up. "Peace, I beg you. For a small, mortal creature it must be difficult to understand but breathe between your words. Have patience."

She rubbed her face in frustration. "What exactly should I do with my time?"

"Read, garden. Walk. Attend the house if you require labour. All the things I do."

"Sounds a bit dull." It was hard not to be petulant.

Crawt stared at her. "I'm offering you my home. Dull? This would be a paradise for many. I am a demon, guardian of the passage to the underworld." His voice grew loud. "My magic sustains all around you, I defend the mortal realm. Dull?" His eyes burnt.

Silence sat between them as she held her breath and finally spoke. "Yes. For a little while."

Crawt almost smiled and shook his head. "Young creatures. You long for adventure?"

"I've killed men and evaded robbers and bandits. Men who'd cut my throat simply because I was there. I've lived on fear and rabbits for months. I've lost everyone I've ever loved. I have nothing and no one. I'm not foolish enough to pass this up. But it might take some getting used to. I miss tea. And cheese. I miss eggs and the sounds of chickens in the yard." Her voice trailed off.

He shrugged his mouth down in thought, slowly nodding. "I do lead a very small existence, but I have so much to do. I can perhaps attend to some of those things."

"I wasn't asking."

"I know." His red eyes were reassuring as he looked back up at her, his dour look melting, and it disconcerted her. "Would you care for some wine? I have a barrel."

"I've never really drunk wine."

He grinned. The fine scars highlighted on his face, and his fangs were on display. She wondered what he used them for, and then remembered that he was vegetarian.

He disappeared and reappeared with a jug and two cups. She smelt the offered wine, finding it dark and thick, and tasted it. She coughed at the sharp sensation at the back of her throat and then drank it.

"It's good."

With a nod, he drank his own.

They sat by the stove as it radiated warmth and drank.

She told him stories of her brothers, and the little tricks and games they would play. How they exasperated their mother and amused their father.

He listened, eyes always on her, and the red depths no longer disconcerting.

She giggled, red-faced and with an empty cup. Her laughter trailed off, and she stared into nothing.

"I think it's time to rest."

She nodded, and he followed her up to bed. He hovered on the landing with the torch, as if he would say something, but he turned, leaving her in darkness. She was alone as Fox stayed curled up by the warm stove.

A garden wall crumbled and fell, Crawt looked at it mournfully and threw off his tunic in the sun to work. Rosalin looked up from the weeds and watched.

His body was a mangle of scars over hard muscle, and she couldn't look away from the glittering patterns on them, or the way he moved as he worked. He picked out the stones and rebuilt the wall, carefully attending his task, and she completely forgot about turning the soil.

He stood up and stretched his back before turning when he'd finished and caught her staring.

They looked at each other for a minute before Crawt grabbed his tunic, and pulling it on, he went inside.

Rosalin didn't move until Crow cawed, and she went back to work, thinking about the past weeks.

Days had passed, weeks grew in number. They'd found a routine. Crawt procured chickens from somewhere, and they pecked happily in the yard as Fox watched them with interest. He never went for them, and Rosalin gave him boiled eggs.

She tended the ever-abundant gardens, ground grain for flour, and cooked. She minded the house and cleaned when she cared to. She sewed herself clothes from cloth Crawt gave her, even choosing a dress for the

warmer weather. She'd worn nothing but trousers and tunic for months. Becoming the young woman again soothed her and reminded her of who she was. The enchanted strangeness became normal. Thought of evil and toil in the world beyond stretched out behind her like a dream.

There was peace, the feel of it crept up on her, and though she had nightmares, or slept fitfully, stillness stole on her, and she was finally ready for it. The sweet air and warm sun reminded her of being a man again. Oddly, so did Crawt.

Paradise was almost like home, but Rosalin closed her eyes and smelt blood and smoke as tension sent her rigid, ready to attack.

Standing, she dropped her trowel. She needed trees and the closeted darkness in the woods. There were times when she hated it, and others when they were the only things that gave her solace. She picked up her light cloak from beside her, and left Fox asleep on the grass.

She knew which paths to take, and where not to stray. Following her favourite, she meandered along and thought about her father. The last moments of his face before covering him over him in dirt shuddered through her.

Rosalin paid no attention to her surroundings, only to her thoughts, and stumbling a little, she blinked in the dim light, finding herself cold and surrounded by unfamiliar dark trees. Turning back, she didn't recognise the way but headed on, brushing brittle, low branches from her face. One snapped, and the jagged edge sprang back, cutting her cheek. She winced and hissed, wiping the scratch as she went.

The further she went, the less she knew where she was.

Trying not to panic, she called out to Fox or Crow and heard nothing. They were often with her, and though Crawt had not explained them, she was sure they guarded her and kept her safe.

She called Crawt's name and waited in the silence, shivering.

In the distance, she saw movement and was sure she saw a flash of horns and a great figure moving.

"Crawt!" Her voice didn't carry, the sound dull as she spoke. She headed to him, relief flooding her, only to find him gone when she neared the spot where he was.

The light faded further, and her breath misted in the cold. She squinted as she turned.

Glancing down, her feet sticking in the mud, she saw no leaves or bracken on the ground, only rank goo. The trees around her were blackened and dead. Terror rose up her throat as he realised how far she'd strayed from the path.

Pulling her foot up, she lost her boot and fell over.

She managed to get up, wiping the dirt off her. It smelt like no mud she'd ever known, almost like decaying meat. She tried to go back, but the trees were denser, and she was sure they had moved. Rosalin felt odd, the world spun and warped around her.

Blinking her focus, movement ahead caught her attention in the dark. Not Crawt, something else. Her mind recoiled.

The thing turned and shaking her head, Rosalin ran, ran as far as she could, leaving her boots in the mire, and went as fast as the ground allowed, as she slid and skidded all the way. Her old instincts kicking in as she moved.

Before she processed any thoughts, she met a wall. A Crawt shaped wall. Rosalin made a strangled sound, and tipped her head back, meeting his angry face as she clung to him. Her rushed breaths and panicked eyes locked onto him.

He picked her up but tensed with a growl at something behind her and set her down again. "Stay," he grunted.

She shuddered and huddled in on herself as he ran into the place where the other creature waited and watched it unfold. She didn't want to see it, fear compelled her to run, but Crawt always drew her.

He put his arms out, and light emanated from him, two long swords materialised bathed in pale blue light, and he wielded them against the creature. The other monster was like him, but completely white, horns longer, with blood smeared over him.

The two clashed and fought. Crawt moved with grace and speed, and as he crouched down, he ran a sword in a diagonal motion, slicing the beast in half. It made a high cry and split into two pieces, and it fell, casting a look to her as the red light went from its eyes.

Crawt stood slowly, the swords vanished, and the light dimmed. He appeared out of the darkness, his face blank, and eyes dull.

Rosalin couldn't make any sound, and her eyes fixed on Crawt, sorrow and anger filling his face. It radiated off him as he picked her up again and took her home. Rosalin finally wept.

Tears and sobs shook her body. She clung to Crawt with her head against his neck. She cried for the horror she'd seen, for the sadness in Crawt. For her father and mother. She wept for her fallen brothers and her home. For the things she had done, and the people she killed.

Rosalin was sorry for it all.

Crawt said nothing, and the motion of walking and his warmth lulled her, and in exhaustion, she closed her eyes to the world and it went dark.

Chaos

Crawt spoke. "Open your eyes."

Rosalin did and found herself in her bed, the fire high with early morning sun streaming through the window. Her throat was dry, and she was dizzy.

Crawt helped her sit and with one hand cupping the back of her head, he put a cup of water to her lips. "How do you feel?"

"Like I've been ill." She touched her sore cheek as she sat back and found it nearly healed.

"You've had a fever for two days. It broke." He placed his hand on her brow, and she relaxed.

Her last memory came back, and she shivered. "What happened?"

He sat back. "I should ask you the same question."

Rosalin blushed with shame. "My mind wandered, and I must have strayed. I couldn't find my way and got more lost with every step. I thought I saw you. What was that? Why did you kill it?"

Crawt turned away for a moment, and Fox jumped on the bed.

With no expression on his face or kindness in his voice, Crawt faced her. "You should leave here."

The fire popped in the silence, and Rosalin nodded as something clenched inside. The horror of the woods sat heavy, and her impulse to flee made her itch, but with him she was safe. She deserved no better than to be sent away. She'd disobeyed his single request. "May I have a few days to regain my strength first?" As much as she wanted to look at him, she didn't.

"Of course." He stood and left the room.

Rosalin hated the cold he left behind, and that she'd lost her strange and only friend.

Fox whined, and she petted his muzzle. Rosalin sought to find the hardness of her heart again. She couldn't right then.

A day passed, and restless by the second, Rosalin packed her things, readied, and found Crawt at the wood store. She watched him for a moment until Crow called.

"You're going now?" Not looking at her, he swung the axe up and over.

"Yes."

Crawt's reply was to swing the axe again, splintering the wood, and the sound of it was sharp. He tossed the logs into the mountain of wood and turned to her. "You have some supplies?"

"Yes, thank you." Rosalin met his cold face with her own. She refused to beg or plead, but the words were on her tongue.

She wore her leather trousers again and left the dress neatly folded in her room. Her new boots, which appeared outside at her door that morning were tight, and she wondered where he got them.

He looked at her feet, and stepping to him, she nearly said asked to stay. With grim understanding, she knew if she survived the journey to the coast, she'd probably meet some other unpleasant end. How many times would she escape fate?

Rosalin glanced beyond Crawt to the dark wood in the distance and swallowed. The thing that Crawt killed haunted her dreams. It whispered death and fear. Every time she blinked, she saw it. The dread stayed with

her, unfading from her mind, and with clarity, she knew death would come soon.

Taking a step back, Rosalin clenched her jaw, and all the muscles in her body tightened. Ah, there it was; the cold hardness she used to survive.

"I'm sorry. I never meant to go against your instruction, and thank you for giving me some rest, and peace. Your kindness means a lot to me."

Crawt growled, swinging axe around and down to a large log, shattering it, and he tossed the pieces aside. His anger deflated, and he frowned with a nod. "Fox will guide you as far as he can. It might be dangerous. Take care."

Rosalin huffed. "You don't need to worry about me. I'm stronger than I look."

After a moment, Crawt wedged the axe in the block with a thump, and went back to the forest, leaving her behind without a glance.

Rosalin watched him retreat before leaving the magical place where she'd found peace.

Fox padded alongside through the gardens. She followed him down the overgrown path to the river. A branch barred the way, and she cut it with her newly sharpened short sword, relishing the weight of it in her hand, or tried to at least.

Crow flew overhead. They marched at a good pace down as the river narrowed and wound back to the forbidden place.

Fox padded across a stone crossing over the fast but shallow water, and she followed him. He sat facing the lighter greener trees, though no path was there.

"I'm to go on alone now?" She knelt and scratched his ears.

Fox lay down.

"Goodbye, Fox." She patted his head and with a deep breath and no plan and went on.

Rosalin blinked at the burning in her eyes and fought the weight in her heart as she did. Crow cawed behind her, his cry growing quiet as she marched until there was only her.

Rosalin marched for days after finding the Gelthan Road, winding north and west finally, skirting the woods as she went. She slept in short bursts, eating meagrely, slipping into her old self with each step.

At last, there was the crossroads village at the head of the road, before it branched into smaller paths, leading her home, or what was left. She entered the re-emerging community with buildings under construction, taking the bustle and noise of industry. She made her way to a rudimentary inn, full of people, and the warm smell of food and ale greeted her as she entered. No one took notice of her.

She ordered food and wine and sat wearily in a dim corner.

The serving girl brought her order and gave her a look. "Where you from?"

"Nowhere, I've travelled a lot."

"South?"

"No. I've not been around people recently, what's the news?"

The girl hesitated and glanced about. "War's over, though the soldiers take what they want and guard the way. Herding people about."

"Why?"

"Make sure nothing starts up again. They need labour." The girl tapped her finger on the table.

"Have you heard of Toolin?"

Her finger stilled. "Nothing there now, as far as I know."

Rosalin nodded. Her home was gone, not that she expected different.

The girl's surliness passed. "A lot of people are looking for new places. Whole cities are gone. The coastal belt is rebuilding but it ain't north friendly. We're all beginning again, best we can. You can do worse than here. But be aware of the soldiers, they pass through now and again."

"Thank you. I will." From her purse, Rosalin threw a coin on the table, and the girl took it with a smile.

She passed the afternoon watching the people come and go, getting used to others again. As the day drew on and she was thinking of where she would sleep, a group of soldiers came into the inn. A hush fell over the patrons.

A fine-looking man leading the group scanned the faces, and landing on hers, his demeanour changed.

Captain Henson.

Rosalin marked his tarnished armour and haggard appearance. He rested his hand on his sword hilt and bore a stern look as he walked over.

"Well, there you are." He smirked.

"Captain."

"You disobeyed me. Why did you run?" Though he laughed a little, his cold eyes made her shrink.

"I decided not to."

"Word also reached us of dead soldiers in the woods. Several. All robbed. The thing about war being over is that order is restored. Clearing the forest of thieves, making the roads safe again. These are my tasks." He stood straight as his bed stood behind him, barring the way.

It was up, and she knew it.

"Seems a menial task, this far north for a fine captain to be assigned to. I wonder why. Though, I did hear tales of a boy with his head on a pike. What was it? You fell over in the blood?"

Henson's face contorted into anger, and with a jerky nod, two soldiers grabbed her, pulling her out from the table, searched her, and found her coin purse and weapons. The soldier's short sword clattered as it a soldier threw it onto the table. Silence pressed in.

"Take her."

Dragged from the inn, she didn't resist and caught sight of the serving girl, who had pitying eyes.

With her wrists tightly bound, a soldier shoved her up into a cart. A leery man sat opposite her. As they bound her legs to the wagon, the familiar deadness ate her up, and the peace Crawt brought her left her mind. They'd kill her, of that she was sure.

They headed south in the morning, and hunger gnawed as she watched the scenery pass.

Rosalin closed her eyes and thought of Crow and Fox, and of the garden, and Crawt's laugh and surly irritation. The sun on her face as she tended the vegetables. The chickens that laid the most delicious eggs. The last sight of Crawt and his disappointment in her. She wanted to beg him to forgive her and go home.

They halted as evening fell, and as the soldiers stretched and started a fire, a crow cawed as it landed in a tree, observing her. Rosalin stopped working her bindings and watched it, smiling as the light faded.

A soldier untied her feet and led her by the rope that bound her wrists, taking her to Henson.

"I have an offer to make you," he said, wiping his sword down. It glinted in the firelight.

Shoved down onto the ground, she was grateful it was at least warm, and the other soldiers left them alone.

"What offer?" She watched him sheath the sword and eat and drink while her bound hands sat in her lap. The minutes drew out.

"You're a pretty thing. Bit thin. Not as much as you once were though. Been well fed wherever you were."

Rosalin kept her face very still and neutral.

"But, there's something about you." He finally paid her attention, and her stomach lurched.

Rosalin kissed a young man once and hoped he'd be her sweetheart, but nothing came of it, and then he died in the war. She'd never been that interested in men other than him, and even then it was only a vague

inclination. She didn't want to be acquainted with Henson that way at all. "You'd force me?"

"Force? No. I should hang you, along with that one," he nodded behind her at the man still in the cart, "but, I don't know for sure that it was you who killed those soldiers. The forest is vast, and there are other bandits out there, yet you have a sword of ours." He frowned a little, lounging back. "Tell me how you acquired it."

There was no point arguing the fact she was not a bandit. She had killed those soldiers.

Rosalin twisted her numb hands, wrists chaffing against the rope. "I found it."

"I can smell a liar from a mile away, and you reek."

"I took it while your men slept."

He sneered. "For all I know, you're the one killing my men in the West forest."

Rosalin looked up. Unease crept up her back, but she kept her face blank, watching him.

"Have you ever set foot in it?" He tilted his head.

"I'd never be so foolish."

"You don't believe all that nonsense?" he scoffed.

"Sometimes, Captain, it pays to listen to the wisdom of others. Myths come from truth." She frowned and shifted, still twisting her wrists, the binds cut in and itched.

"I can cut them off."

Rosalin stilled. "You want a sex worker, only I wouldn't get paid. And you think I'll be grateful to you for not killing me."

"I need company."

"If I refuse?"

"You hang. If you say yes, you get hot water to wash in and food."

"How long do I have to think about it?" The light failed utterly, the gloaming passing from around her, leaving her cold, which did nothing to ease her aching body.

"We always hang at dawn."

She already knew her choice because there wasn't one. Who was she to be proud? She'd stay alive.

Rosalin stared into the flames for a while. Absently, she heard the crow caw, and her eyes closed at the sound. It comforted her.

A commotion at the other end of the camp made her swing around and look into the dimness beyond, Henson already on his feet and sword in hand, stepped forward past the flames to see better. Screams came from the darkness, and he stepped back.

Two tall, white creatures with curling black horns and red eyes appeared. Rosalin's mouth hung open as she shook her head. The first leant forward, focused on her, while the second caught a soldier and snapped his neck.

Henson stood frozen to the spot and dropped his blade, and Rosalin dived onto it, cutting her binds. The two demons advanced, but at a roar behind them, they turned. Blue light gleamed as Crawt emerged.

He circled the demons, and lunged, missing his mark as one jumped onto his back. He roared as he bit him. Crawt slashed at the second creature before throwing off the one on his back. Glittering blue blood poured from a wound on his neck.

Rosalin grabbed the sword, hands prickling and heart pounding, and charged, slashing the back of the demon as it rose to its feet. It turned and struck out with its claws, slicing her tunic and skin. It stung and burnt. Nausea crawled up her throat, and she dropped the sword. Crawt took its head off, his swords bright in the dark, ringing in a clean tone.

The two demons lay dead along with all the soldiers.

Henson knelt, face agog.

Crawt turned to Rosalin and retracted his swords. "You cannot go five minutes unsupervised."

Rosalin put her hand to her chest and looked at the blood on her fingers. Her relief at seeing him was stayed.

Crawt glanced at the captain. "I came for two reasons. Those things that murdered your men, and you. I know all depravity of mortals. I have seen untold evil. You'd make her a toy for your sport."

Henson stared into Crawt's eyes, the red in them glowed, and as Crawt put his hand to the man's head, Rosalin retched.

"I have unmade men over thousands of years for the same crimes that you commit. I have turned their souls to dust and from the bones, built monsters of them. I have not the time, but it is what you deserve."

Henson began to cry. An ugly sobbing. Crawt pulled him up, holding him. Henson whimpered but didn't fight.

"I know what you have done. A child you murdered, his headless body left to rot, begging for his life as you took it. Women raped. Houses burnt. The damage you have wrought deserves penance."

Henson's body sank in on itself with a crack. Bones broke, blood pooled under him.

Rosalin covered her mouth to muffle a cry.

Crawt dropped the dead man and spoke to her, fire burning in him. "Now you see me for what I really am. I am the monster. I am the thing from tales told to children. You know what my name was?" he spat.

Crawt grabbed the body and dragged it, hauling it up to the cart. He began adding the other soldiers.

"I am a devil, one of many. A legion of our kind exists," he growled as he worked. "The things and life and torment I could give to these bodies," he gestured at the heap of the dead, "would destroy your soul if you knew. I answer to an evil power that seeks to dole out torture and pain. The tales you have spoken of are not wholly wrong. Nor is it the truth."

He set the cart of bodies on fire and heaved the demons on top.

Rosalin fell prostrate, squinting at the fire, repulsed by the smell, and she wheezed. "You came."

Crawt knelt next to her, pulling her up to him, holding her gently. "Yes, you were in danger. Are you injured? How?"

Rosalin swallowed hard and took deep breaths with gritted teeth, pain stabbing in her chest. "Its claws. Help me." She held her fists to her chest.

He prised a hand from her and shook his head at the wound with a growl. "Hold tight."

Crow took flight and vanished into the air, his call echoing. The air was thick and acrid with smoke as Crawt pressed her to his chest as he stood. She didn't flinch, and Rosalin was sucked away, falling into an endless whirl of darkness.

Choice

Pain. All Rosalin knew was pain, and it radiated out from her chest. She tried to move but was trapped. Making a strangled noise, the hold on her eased.

"You are safe. I need to clean your wound."

Rosalin leant away from Crawt's hold. "What happened?"

Light appeared around her as lamps flickered into life in the kitchen, and Crawt set her on a chair by the pump. She pulled off her jacket and opened the tie of her tunic with a grimace. Under her neck, thick gouges throbbed. He knelt beside her and cleaned them with blessedly cold water. She jumped at the sting.

"I felt you. Your distress." He glanced up.

"How?"

He grunted and kept dabbing with a cloth. "Then there are other things. Demons are wandering beyond this place. They shouldn't be able to."

"They came for me."

He didn't reply.

"Why did you kill the captain?"

Crawt opened a foul-smelling stone jar and scooped out a pale blue salve. "This might hurt."

At first the paste was cool, but a tight sensation radiated through her flesh. Rosalin winced. It stung and started to burn. Pin prickling and scratching in her chest intensified. She hissed and squirmed.

Crawt held her still, and she met his eyes, furious pain stealing her breath.

"The captain killed the last of a line of kings, and it ended a kingdom and the war. No more kings. The price of his crime was exile as demanded by the new dominion. Those people have pillaged and destroyed the lives of every town and village from here to the mountains of the north where no men dwell. No farm or community has been left untouched. They have razed your home to the ground. I never look beyond my walls." He leant his head forward, searing her with his glowing eyes. "I never gaze beyond my realm to that of people, for it is violent and bloody and makes me doubt my path. The will of people is a cruel, hateful thing. I was curious about you and your story, so I looked. Then there is you."

Rosalin, captivated, whimpered at the pain. "What did you put on me?"

Crawt held her tighter. "They have your scent. They want you. You are marked now."

Rosalin couldn't breathe, and tears ran down her face. "Why do they want me? Who are they?"

"My kind loathe me because I took power from them. You are a mortal, and they devour mortals. This is my fault."

The pain ebbed, and she relaxed. The scratches were warm, and as he let go, she felt the fresh red scar tissue. She looked back up, and his own wound had healed.

The lamps flickered, and fox padded over, putting his head on her knee. Crawt sat back. "You should bathe and rest."

"Thank you for coming for me. I'm sorry for all the trouble I've given."

"Sorry? I have done this. I am not sure how to fix it. I thought sending you away was for the best. To keep you safe."

She smiled in fluttering relief and went to bed.

Rosalin put on her dress again, after enjoying a bath in the morning, and found Crawt in the early pink dawn where she left him. With a deep frown, he gazed out the window.

"Crawt?"

"How do you feel?" He didn't move.

"Better." Other than the horrific nightmares.

A strange expression passed over him, as if wrestling with something, finally it eased, and he looked at her with pity. "The underworld is filled with horror. It wants out. You are caught in a war you can't understand. There is no escape for you."

"I've survived this long." Rosalin busied herself and tidied up.

"You have a choice. An impossible one. Come with me. I want to show you something." He faced her, and she couldn't read his expression.

She followed him outside, and he led her through the garden, down to the river, but instead of following the path, he walked through another hidden way. They wound through rich foliage and up, the morning wearing away until they reached the crest of a hill opening out to hot sun. In the middle was a low stone table, covered in lichen and moss, shaded by an ancient oak.

He took a massive slow breath, and his mood broke. "Beneath this world is another. I keep what lives there at bay. They will keep trying, but I will not let them. There is only one thing I can do to keep you safe. Give you power."

With a frown, he beckoned her to follow. They made their way down, and through denser undergrowth, they came to a pool. A light stream pattered down through rocks into clear water.

"This is beautiful."

"It is. I should have sent you away the moment I found you in my chair. A mortal in my home was..." Crawt turned from the water and lifted his head to the sky. "I must put this right, but every choice leads to your death. I am damned for everything I do. It is the price of my power, and now we face

another choice. Do I let them take you and devour your soul, or do I damn you to my fate?"

Her heart skipped. "Do not let them take me. I'll do anything."

"Anything? Mortals have no concept of consequences. You see only your small lives." His eyes glowed as he faced her and sneered.

"Then what do I do? What will this mean?"

"To take what power I have is to surrender yourself to magic, but you are infected by it already. It is why they want you." With a pained face, he looked down.

He closed his eyes and crouched down, dipping his hand in the water, murmuring words, and the water rippled. Birds raised from the trees and flew into the air.

"Crawt?"

"Would you offer yourself to me willingly? Would you choose this monster?"

Rosalin took a sharp breath as she understood what he was asking of her and offering to give her. "Yes." There was no hesitation in her mind.

He bowed his head. "Swim."

Rosalin glanced at the water before stripping. Crawt kept his eyes lowered as she made her way into the water. She shivered and dipped under for a moment.

Crow cawed and took flight, and Fox, who'd kept close, scampered out of sight.

"You will be bound to what I am. Your fate is tangled with mine."

Rosalin's heart thumped. "What else?"

"You will no longer be a mortal, and beyond that, I do not know. There is no precedent for this. Last night I thought as the stars turned, of all the ways to spare you, and there is none other than this."

"Then do it."

He slumped his shoulders and undressed but met her stern eye. A powerful, deeply scarred creature faced her. The intricate patterns that ran through the scars of his body caught the light, and he was magnificent to see.

All thought left her, and she just kept breathing.

Crawt stepped into the water, his frame wading through where she didn't reach the bottom. Facing him as he approached, she wasn't afraid, not like with Henson.

"It's not too late. You can refuse."

"What will happen if we do not?"

He appeared helpless.

"Wait, wait. What does it mean for you?" When he didn't answer, she asked again.

"My power will protect you. We will be one."

Rosalin's breath came sharp and quick. "You don't want that, do you?"

"I vowed never, I made it so this was forbidden, but I vowed many things. My power is vast. My responsibility heavy. My burdens are not for you, nor would I have them so. But I am responsible for this. It is my fault."

"Crawt, I don't understand, but maybe we shouldn't do this." Rosalin swam closer.

"I am the embodiment of magic, and the form you see is the magic itself. I made this place, myself, and all rules here. I dictate, and only I can change it. I will change it." As he spoke, his presence expanded, and his voice resonated and echoed. He bared his fangs in the silence.

In the hot sun, Rosalin went cold and trembled.

She bowed her head in understanding. His very flesh was power. She would be part of that.

"Then I will do my best to be whatever you need." Rosalin summoned her courage and lifted her face. A calm realisation that she welcomed this swept over her, and she smiled.

Crawt moved closer, frowning and unsure, and his hands went to her waist pulling her near.

"Will it hurt?" she whispered.

"Yes. I cannot imagine it would not. I'll be as kind as I can. I have never done this."

Crawt ran a finger along the point of his horn, and blood dripped from a small cut. A few drops dispersed in the water and the colour began to change. All around her darkened, and the pool became inky.

He put his finger to Rosalin's forehead and murmured again, running his finger in circles. He drew little patterns on her that mirrored his own. Down her face and neck, shoulders and arms. She lifted one and put it on his shoulder, and he drew the language of magic on her. Then the other arm.

The intricate patterns of blood dried instantly, and the markings burnt and tingled. He turned her gently and did the same to her back.

Dipping low with his free arm, he lifted her up and continued down her back. Back in the water, he turned her again, lifted her, and did the same to her breasts.

The sun beat down on them, the water warmed. Rosalin relaxed, lulled by the deep murmuring of words she didn't understand.

His fingers brushed against her nipple, and his voice faltered.

Their eyes met, and his were on fire as she wrapped her legs around his hips. She felt a hard length pressing against her.

Crawt lifted her bottom a little, and holding her cheeks, pressing slightly into her.

Rosalin froze at the feeling; he seared her.

Pressing into his chest, she clung on. "Do it."

"I am sorry." Holding tight he thrust up to her, and she screamed. Her head fell back as she gasped for breath. It was wrong and painful, and she knew they had broken some vow, some dictate. A person and a demon together, and with one so powerful, there would be consequences.

Crawt didn't move but held her tight with controlled strength and scent of sun and fresh water on his skin.

The initial pain subsided, and he was merely hot inside her. Stretching and intruding.

"Crawt?" she whispered into his neck.

He didn't speak, but she felt him shudder, and leaning back, she tried to look at him, but he turned his face away.

"Look at me."

Crawt did. The light had gone from his eyes, and tears fell. He adjusted his hold, but she wouldn't wince. She wiped the tears from him, holding back her own.

"I'm not that bad, am I?" She tried to smile.

Taking a deep breath, he rested his forehead on hers. "No."

With that, he moved gently. He kissed her cheek with a sweetness she'd not expected but relished, and his lips were full and soft. His skin wasn't rough against hers either, and he was a contradiction. For a moment, she wondered at her own heart for welcoming him, but she clung tighter, losing herself to the feel of his tenderness.

Rosalin moaned, and it didn't feel terrible. With each soft glide into her, pleasure and desire spiralled. Crawt's breath became ragged, and he growled, holding her tighter.

Where he'd marked her with his blood, grew warmer again, every mark became sensitive, and a strange feeling spread over her. She gasped as the sensations increased. The intense need peaked, sending her mind blank. For that moment, she was strung out through time, eternal, and knew all pain and all pleasure.

Crying loudly as her body became something more than it was, she convulsed in his hold. He thrust hard into her and squeezed her as he found his own release. He held her as it ebbed away, and Rosalin returned to her mind.

Crawt leant back and studied her face.

Rosalin panted and smiled, but he didn't.

He pulled her off him and set her in the water. The loss of him left her cold.

The black water dissipated and became clear again, the marks on her skin washed away. Breathless, body still taut with pleasure, she wanted to reach out to him.

"Was that... I mean, what happens now?" She swam nearer.

"Nothing. That was it."

"Will I change, become like you?"

"What if you did?" Crawt moved back.

"I wouldn't care."

He huffed and swam back to the shore, leaving her bereft.

"I wouldn't. It's better than whatever awaited me." She followed him.

He heaved up from the water and stood with his back to her, light catching the scars. What pain had he endured? She wanted to comfort him.

"You'd give up all your beauty?"

"Beauty? I don't know about that. Crawt, that was magical. A bit painful at first, but you were lovely. That was... I can't even think of the word." Heat filled her face.

He turned, and she didn't hide looking him over as she neared the shore. Crawt pulled his breeches on.

"It was an act of magic to keep you safe. I do care about you, of course, and it is not something I do lightly. You cannot understand what this means for you." He didn't look at her as he dressed.

Angry, she snapped, climbing out the water. "Then explain it. Why did you weep?"

"For you. For what might come. For what I have done. I have defiled that which I swore never to."

"You didn't defile me. I chose." She stepped closer, not caring she was nude.

"You chose poorly," he shouted, face contorted.

"You told me I had no choice." She bit out. The hot sun warmed her wet skin as it dripped. He glanced down her body.

"This is impossible."

"Why, because I'm mortal?"

He kept looking at her, but she didn't waver under his fierce stare, if anything it compelled her.

"I thought you said-"

Baring his fangs, he growled. "I don't know what will happen. I cannot see all. I am sure of some things, but this is forbidden. I have defied every law of the realm I set down the laws to." He sighed, anger spent as he thrust her dress at her. "Cover yourself."

"Why don't you explain? I'm tired of cryptic half-truths." She tried to keep her temper as she dressed in sharp, angry movements.

"I've not had to explain my actions to another, ever. I could undo everything by doing this, and yet I knew it was the only way. I am sorry for it." He turned from her, and the sadness in his voice hurt.

Crawt led, and Fox stayed near. Her legs ached, and she struggled with each step as they headed up the hill to the clearing. Her mind went over every word and what they shared, trying to understand his anger.

The heat overcame her when they reached the top, and she sat on the dry grass, nausea crawling up her throat.

The stone table blurred, and in her vision, a thousand blue butterflies danced. They descended and swam about in the air around her. Stretching out her hand, they landed on her fingers and arm and swarmed in her damp hair.

Crawt brushed them away and knelt.

"Rosalin?" His voice was distant.

"Perhaps you were right, and this was a mistake."

Crawt bowed his head, as if in prayer, and then hauled her up, placing her on the table. Butterflies scattered and regrouped.

He put his hand to her forehead, the marks returning to her skin as he did.

"Rosalin." His voice reverberated through her.

Opening her eyes, she winced at the light with her head pounding. "What's happening?"

"What I feared." He ran his hand over her eyes, and she sighed. The dark felt like home. She knew it and always had. The darkness wasn't new to her, it was her own and rose to the surface, expanding through her. It was what let her kill and spurred her to survive.

Pain shot through her body, and her heart grew hot. Her skin became tight as pressure expanded inside until so intense, she screamed, writhing to escape. In her mind, she saw time and change all around her. She saw darkness, felt heat, and heard screams. Strength filled her limbs as the pain left an echo when it ebbed.

The butterflies danced away on the breeze, and she looked at Crawt. He staggered back from her.

"What is it?" she asked, her voice slow and odd to her ears.

"What I have I done?"

"I feel it. Am I different?" She looked at her arms, pushing up her sleeves, she saw the same fine markings that Crawt bore were now hers. Her skin was no longer pink and pasty, but a pale grey. Rosalin felt her face, she had no horn or fang and felt the same as it ever did. She bore an echo of the magic that made him. Grabbing her hair, she strained to see it, pulling it forward, it was no longer brown, but a strange almost blue colour.

"Is it so bad?" she whispered as she smoothed her hair and looked at her arms again.

"No, you are beautiful. But I have taken something beautiful from you."

She smiled at his pained and drawn face. "Don't be sorry. I have an ugly soul. I see it now. I'm a murderer. Cold. Unfeeling."

"You are not unfeeling, Rosalin." He sounded so sad and weary.

"I think this has cost you more than you are willing to say."

He made no answer.

"I'm sorry you are upset, but I'm not sorry I am here and with you. How can I be?"

"Come, let's go home." He helped her up, supporting her all the way back, and it felt right.

Sore between her legs, she wondered what would happen now. Rosalin knew her heart, and that he held some tenderness beyond pity for her, why else do the one thing he vowed not to?

Rosalin had hope.

History

✳

Rosalin scrubbed and wrung linens and rinsed the stones with the wash water. She glanced up and saw Crawt watching. A whole week and he avoided her. She only saw him at meals, and then he'd skulk off. Her hope quickly dwindled.

She looked at her hands as they caught the sun, glittering patterns just like his. She was part of him. Not that he cared.

Crawt hovered in the line of trees, shook his head, but then strode over to her. She turned the wash barrel over to dry.

"Rosalin." He scowled.

She only looked at him.

"You've been cleaning."

Crow cawed from somewhere, and Crawt pressed his lips into a line and turned briefly as if to scold the bird.

"I like to keep busy, seeing as you want nothing to do with me, and I need some occupation."

"I've been remiss."

"Yes."

He opened his mouth and closed it again. "Come. You've done enough."

She had. Windows scraped and cleaned, floors, fireplaces, rugs were beaten of dust, weeds pulled; the list went on.

Crawt led her to the library, and fox trotted into the house with them, and Crow joined his master, briefly perching on Crawt's horn before he shooed him off and the bird flew through the house.

In the library, the bird squawked, and Crawt gave it a dry look as they followed him in.

She wondered what they were saying to each other, but she didn't ask just as she didn't ask all the other questions that burnt in her.

Crawt started a fire and poured her a glass of wine. She turned the fine goblet in her hands. She'd never had glasses at home, just tin cups.

He hovered and left but came back with some food. He sat opposite and ate a little, opened his mouth to speak, sighed and sat back.

"Say it." Rosalin petted Fox as he sat nearby.

"It is strange to see another like me, not wholly, of course, but we bear the same power." He nodded as if deciding something.

"You've been alone for a long time."

"I was a man before there were forests. The world is vast, and all demons were once set in it, but I changed the foundations of reality and trapped my kind. Before that, there were wars, and death, and mortals were fodder." He waved the conversation off. "Other than for my companions and the rogue demons that escape the underworld, I have nought but myself. Seeing what I have done to you, and that you are here at all... time is not the same for me as it is for you. Does it feel long since you've been here?" He leant forward, scrutinising her face.

"Yes."

"Hmm." He drank his wine.

Rosalin perched on the edge of the chair, shuffling closer to him and reached out her hand, so she nearly touched his knee. "What happened at

the pool made me see. In the weeks that I've been here, I've come to care for you."

The fire crackled a little in the fading day, and he went to speak but only shifted away. Heat filled her face, and she closed her eyes.

He stood before the books. "This is my history. It is in the language that marks our skin." He pulled an ancient book from the shelf and the binding split. "I keep it because there is no witness." Crawt ran his hand down the broken spine as the book crumbled in his hold. "I loved a mortal woman once and what happened led me to this, but it was never what I wanted. Do you understand?"

"No."

"I was not as you see," he gestured to himself, "I was a lesser demon. We are greyish, smaller, mangled copies of the first demons. I crawled out of the earth and filth in exile and was here. People happened upon me. They tortured me. A woman, Mirelda the fair they called her, tended my wounds. I had a little power then. I manipulated her, and everyone else. As punishment, I stripped them of everything they possessed. I'd beguiled Mirelda, and she followed me.

"We wandered all the lands and settled. I built a home, and I would not have her. She was perfect, and I refused to soil her goodness with my evil."

"She loved you."

"She did. Believed I could be redeemed, or that I was enchanted." Crawt closed his eyes with a small smile on his lips and then grew solemn. "A group from the town followed and searched us out. They came in the night and took her from her bed. I can still hear her screams. They took me outside and hanged me. I cannot die. I swung from the tree with my neck broken.

"They killed her and took everything. I could not help her."

Rosalin swallowed her tears for him and for the long-dead Mirelda.

Crawt took a deep breath, sat back down, still holding the remnants of the book, and drank his wine before continuing. "A night passed, and I felt

my body force itself back together, I regained the use of my arms and pulled up the rope. It was agony, and yet I did not really feel it. I managed to get free and once on the floor, I could heal properly, and I went to her. I buried her away from there, under an oak. My anger knew no limit."

His eyes flickered to hers, and they burnt, not just red, but with hate and fire, and dimmed again. "I went deep into the woods and found the place where I crawled out of the earth at the heart of where my kind dwell. There were few passages into the underworld, but when I was cast out, they threw me up into a pit. I was vomited out of it, and it made a hole. When I went back, I begged and pleaded, but they would not hear me, and then I took what I wanted from them. I stole magic and power from that place. There are times when I wonder about what I did, and how. How did I take that power? I wonder now that it was not destiny that brought me to this. My rage was endless, I cursed those who made me, I swore to exact revenge and horror on all; that I would break the structure of my existence, and I dug my hands deep into the source and took all I could. I used what small power I had and claimed everything.

"The pain I cannot describe, and there are no words in any language to recount what I suffered. What I did was unforgivable by our kind, but I stole what was not mine and became a demon master among the first demons. There is no precedent for me."

She looked at him and saw it in her mind, the vision forming with clarity like she had his memory; she understood. A circular stone with a hole in the centre drew up from the filth. Crawt, knee deep, covered in the mire. Smaller, his skin grey, and body scarred.

He said strange words, his eyes completely red, head tipped forward, and his hands reached down into the bottomless power.

The ground shook. Rosalin could smell the damp cloying mud, feel the cold, wet air, and the crackle of power about her. The familiar memory of it

made her feel sick. She felt his rage in her heart and the fury of his unbound grief.

The trees rustled and leaves whispered. All life protested. Crawt screamed as his flesh ripped open and dark blood poured from him.

He pulled his hands away and staggered, falling to his knees as whatever he'd taken consumed his body and changed him utterly. He sank down into the mud. Crawt writhed and sobbed, he begged and pleaded to any that would hear, but the air grew quiet, and the world listened to his horror.

Rosalin felt time pass, long yet swift, and Crawt clawed out, covered in filth. Pulsing blue, he convulsed, eyes aflame, mouth twisted open, and he glowed. A burst of energy shot out from him in a wave, and the ground shook harder as the sky turned black. Glowing and light, his form stretched, pulling him up into the air. He dropped to the ground, hunched like a wounded beast, and roared.

Hours he stayed there, air crackling until the air pressure broke, and rain came. Heavy and cold. Seasons seemed to pass within a storm, thunder rolled as rain pelted down. The only sensation he knew was lingering pain and a steady pulse.

Finally, coming to, Crawt stood wearily with his knees bent and swaying, and in the vision, Rosalin stood with him, the rain chilling her skin. She followed him as he staggered from the now dead forest. The land around him that was once rich with life was dim and withered.

He held out his hand, and turning it, blue light glowed from him. Power too great to be contained, it dripped from his body, and in a clumsy command, he put his arms out, and the rain stopped. The sun rose, and around him, life grew abundant. Spring came in an instant.

In relief of expelling the power that burnt within, he sagged down to his knees and lay on the soft grass.

Cleansed of mud, free from the forest, time passed, and he came to his senses.

All the while Rosalin stood at his side, living his pain and helpless to do anything, but she felt the knowledge within him and understood the power. As Crawt spoke in a murmur, the words appeared on his skin. Cuts appeared and bled over the fresh scars of his transformation, closing quickly. He spoke until he was covered with words of his tongue.

From the newly brightened forest beyond, a fox scampered out. Crawt held his hand out to it, curious, and it padded over. Blue light touched the fox, and for a second, its eyes glowed, but diminished and then it sat.

The vision faded, and Rosalin was in the library with her wine again. She drank it in one long series of gulps.

Crawt was staring at her. "You saw it?"

Rosalin opened and closed her fist to steady her hand.

"The condemnation of my kind is always with me, and it grows with each season of the mortal world. I sealed the all the paths that we travelled through, but in doing so, I cracked the divide between realms. The white well you saw is the place where it happened. They resent that what I did and despise that it was me who did it; a mere serf that was a man in another life." He shrugged his mouth down and worried his top lip with his fangs, lost for a moment. Rosalin watched him, fascinated.

"You were a mortal man once?"

He grunted. "Yes. It was hot, and I was a soldier. My body was stripped and destroyed with my soul. They consumed my flesh and remade me. A torture of undoing that lasted an age. The purpose was to punish and make more of our kind. The lines or right and wrong, reasoning and purpose, blurred for the masters but mine never did." He shrugged and poured them each more wine.

"My work is endless. Reality is brittle, so you move a thing that is brittle and fragile, you might crack it, like that glass. Things can squeeze through gaps."

Rosalin frowned, blinking out of the vision. "The west woods. The captain questioned me, and he said men had been vanishing in the forest."

Crawt's face snapped up. "It's worsening as my power is spent. I have guarded the cracks and fissures of the realms. It is my fate, but I am weary and old. There will come a time when I fail."

They were silent for a minute. "Did you ever get revenge?"

He sat back, turning to the fire, the chair creaking under his weight. "No. I cannot leave for any real length of time, the power here is of me, and without me, it fails completely. There is law, and the realms of mortals and demons cannot cross, except for you." He pinned her with a stare. "It is made because I made it. This is the gateway that I guard, and I am its Lord."

Rosalin turned away, she needed air.

Consequences

L eaving Crawt to his books, Rosalin went out. With her heart pinching, she ignored him calling after her, and travelled out to the river and found her way to the hill.

She reached the clearing and the stone table. The great oak creaked and swayed in the breeze. Its branches gnarled and thick, and lush green leaves rustled softly. There was beauty and rest here in the quiet woods and hills, though she found no peace.

This was where he buried Mirelda, and the thought made her smile in her sadness.

She sat looking down, and in the distance, she saw the pool where they were together. That warm memory, full of fear and desire, made her ache. The sun began to set, red and pink light cast over the clearing and she thought.

He was a Lord and guardian to the under-realm of demons, and she loved him. She laughed. It echoed out into the wind.

She heard Crawt approach. He didn't speak, and hating the silence, she turned.

Her blood ran cold.

"It's true," the creature said.

Taller and thinner than Crawt with smooth marble white skin and glossy black horns, which curled and pointed at her. His eyes were as red as Crawt's, burning brightly in the lowering sun. "You are an abomination," he spat.

Rosalin shifted to her knees, heart hammering. "Who are you?"

The creature laughed. "I am Palzine. Though, I expect Crawt has not told you about me. We were brothers once, of a sort. He and I danced among the dead." He enunciated his words through a sharp smile and sharper teeth. There was a smooth ease and charm to him. How odd.

"Brothers?" She looked him up and down.

His sneer could have cut glass. " Perhaps more like my son. I am... a Master of the underworld. Did he claim to be Lord yet? Did he claim his authority? He is a usurper and snake and an expelled lesser demon. Yet, here he is." Palzine turned in a circle, gesturing to everything with his head tipped back. "We've waited for an age for this moment, and now he has given me such a gift." A butterfly danced in the air, and Palzine held a clawed hand out. The butterfly landed and turned black, died, and fell to the ground. Palzine grinned at Rosalin.

He approached, and she moved to a crouch.

"Ah, now, do not think to attempt to run-"

She fled, down into the valley, towards the pool. They came for her. Crawt was right; what he'd done for her had consequences. She prayed to him as her mind raced and reeled. She found power in her desperation that she did not know she possessed. Her legs brought speed, and she cut and weaved through shrubs and trees, and jumped a fallen tree as she headed out into the woods.

Making sure to stay in the light, and veering west, she climbed ground again. She begged Fox and Crow to seek their master.

Three creatures came from a bend in the path, stopping her dead in her tracks.

They were person-sized and twisted, with remnants of southerner uniforms hanging off them in tattered rags. Her mouth twisted open with a cry stuck in her throat. She braced to fight, and with it, a peculiar sensation ran through her arms. Her hands burnt, pain seared her, and white-hot power shot through her upper body, and with a scream, she bore two heavy swords aflame in white-blue fire. Rosalin staggered at the pain that stole her breath, but she kept her footing, fear thick in her mind.

The three creatures winced and stepped back. Rosalin moved forward with tears in her eyes as her arms throbbed and stung, wielding the swords. One raised in a circular motion, she dipped and swung upwards, cutting the head off the nearest with a wrenching cry. The other two approached in unison, and she swept both arms up and inward, slicing them in two before they saw her move. It came naturally to her as it had when she fought for survival in the woods with her father.

She turned, feeling Palzine approach.

"You have more power than I thought, child."

Rosalin heard the familiar cawing of Crow, and Palzine glanced up.

"One of his pets, I believe." Palzine almost sounded bored.

"You're afraid of him."

He bared his teeth and rushed her, taking her by surprise, but she stepped to the side, slicing him as she crouched low, and he pivoted around.

"Do you think a blow from a weapon can best me?" He winced as dark blood oozed from the wound.

"Ordinary swords, no, but this power is not mortal, as you know." Crawt's voice made her heart leap.

Palzine closed his mouth, and with another bored look, glanced up as Crawt leapt down from the hill above, landing behind Palzine with a heavy thud. Reaching his arms out, his swords appeared in bright light, and he gripped them tightly, and Crawt looked dangerous as he approached.

"Crawt, you have gone too far. This abomination needs to come with us, she needs to return below, as do you." Pazline pointed at her.

"No."

"Our Lord-"

Crawt stepped closer, anger burning. "He is not my Lord. I take no instruction from him. I have my own path."

Rosalin stepped back from the fury vibrating between the two demons staring at each other.

"And your path involves defiling the laws that you made, and undoing all of us? How could you give a mortal unadulterated power? Our rules exist for a reason. Your recklessness will undo us all."

"We are irrelevant. We are a relic of another time. This is a mortal world. It is not ours."

Palzine pointed at Rosalin. "They spread like a disease and cover all the lands with no one to keep them in check. We are here to kill millions with plagues and pestilence and to dole out retribution to the fallen of war and death, and yet we cannot because you barred the gates." Palzine glanced at the swords either side of him.

Crawt softened his face. "Do you remember the great feasts at the caverns? How we'd celebrate death and horror? How all depravity was ours. I hated it. I hated what we were, what I was made into, and saw no joy in it, only pain."

For a moment Palzine wavered as the demons stared at each other. "What if you kill me, do you think that will be it? The whole realm is watching you. Come, come home. Speak with us, make a truce." Palzine's sweet, placating voice made Crawt and Rosalin sneer at the same time.

"You think, after coming to kill who is mine, I would go with you?"

"No then?" Palzine looked amused, a glint returning to his eyes and a little smile danced on his lips. Palzine turned to her. "And what of you? Hmm? Would you care to come and play?"

Rosalin said nothing but smiled in return and adjusted her stance. She felt Crawt's eyes on hers, a warning to hold back. In the periphery, as she stared at Palzine, Crawt slowly shifted in readiness. In a blur of movement, and in silence, Crawt circled his swords, and she went low and lunged in response. They both cut Palzine, reducing him into three pieces.

The demon gasped as ooze bubbled from his mouth, and he fell apart in front of them. Crawt and Rosalin stood straight, and their swords vanished, leaving them in dying light.

"Go back with Fox, and I'll take care of this." Crawt stared at the remains.

"No. Whether you wished it or not, I'm in this now. Part of it. We should deal with it together. You forget I've seen things as well."

"You are so young and small. You're also very lovely. It's hard to see you as anything else."

Rosalin smiled then sobered, seeing the black ooze kill the grass around the remains in an instant. "How do we get rid of them?"

"Fire."

At a little clearing, neglected and bare, Rosalin built a fire. Using dead wood from about them, she made a rough platform raised from the ground and stacked branches all around. Crawt brought what remained of the bodies, and they watched them burn from a distance, avoiding the acrid smoke.

"Why fire?"

"So, they don't put themselves back together. It's a universal. Fire kills everything, and allows new growth."

Rosalin took a slow sigh as she nodded, exhausted. "My arms hurt."

"It doesn't go away."

"Perfect."

They waited until they were lumps of ash, and then kicked out the remains until the fire was out. Crawt took her hand and guided her back through the dark.

When they reached the clearing with the stone table, Rosalin broke their silence. "This is where you buried her?"

"Yes."

"I'm sorry."

"She was mortal, and then I was only a lesser demon, but there was little I could do. At least with you, I could do something. You'd have been consumed with disease without the salve. They'd take you with them..."

"Why were you expelled?"

He led her again, taking her hand. "I pleaded for the lives of those we would kill with a particularly vile plague. It would take children mostly. To what end? For the appetites of others, not because it was just. I hated what I was, yet it had a purpose, but what we did, the way it was done, was wrong. I could not continue."

Crawt didn't let go of her hand the whole way back, and she watched him in wonder.

Acquiesce

〈 〉

Crow sat on Crawt's shoulder, squawked, hopped onto his horn and when Crawt shook his head, Crow flapped and landed on fox. Fox barely moved from his spot by the fire in the library.

Rosalin sighed, swinging her leg over the side of Crawt's great chair. Heavy summer rain cleaned the air, watering the crops. She half-watched the rain on the window, not paying attention to the book she was attempting to decipher. She turned back to look at Crawt, who was scratching away with quill and parchment.

"Where do you get your ink?" Rosalin asked.

"I can give you more chores if you are bored," he murmured.

In the awkward time since Palzine, it felt like all she did was chores. "I just want to know how you make it."

"It is my blood because it is magic. Like the salve. And everything else." He said it slowly, still focused on writing.

Rosalin pressed her lips together. "You said you'd teach me how to read this language, but I don't understand it." She waved the book at him.

He put the quill down and ran his tongue over a fang.

She smirked. Irritating him was becoming a habit, being the only attention he gave her. "I'm annoying you again."

"You do not annoy me. I am attempting to rewrite the law I created." He gestured to the wall of books and scrolls. "It is not an easy thing to do."

"Oh. You can do that?"

"Perhaps. I do not really know." He sat back, pressing his hands together. "I have to try."

"Why?"

He growled. "You. Always you."

"Sorry."

"No, I am sorry. It will not end with Palzine. He was important in the hierarchy. More will come, and if they're making those creatures and not taking time to create true demons, then they are desperate. Desperation makes them more dangerous. They want you and will not stop."

Rosalin's hands shook. Crawt crossed the room and knelt by her, and she met his eyes.

"I will do my best to protect you. They were not expecting you to have the power you do. Maybe they thought I'd let you die or let them take you."

"What do we do?"

"Wait. I need to finish this."

"Then I'll leave you to it."

"You do not have to leave, just let me work." Crawt went back to the desk.

He refocused on the desk and scratched away.

"Perhaps I'll pick some mushrooms for dinner, there was a little crop growing in the garden, and they'll be ready today."

"Do not stray from the house and take Crow and Fox."

Crow squawked and flapped up onto Rosalin's shoulder, and Fox padded out.

He called after her. "For pity's sake, be careful."

Picking up a trug, she went out, the rain had stopped, and earthy newness scented the air. She found the little clump and with a knife, cut them, and filled the shallow basket. She picked a few greens and stretched her back.

Crow flapped off and landed on the grass, strutting around looking for his own dinner. Rosalin put the basket down and opened and closed her fists.

The strange discomfort of power was a constant ache. She held her arms out and let it come. A sharp press under her flesh and the swords appeared. Heavy, bright and pale blue. She closed her hand around the hilt in her fist.

She couldn't drop them, but she could shift her grip.

"Do you wish to practise?"

She smiled before turning. "Did you think I was in trouble?"

"I always think you are in trouble."

She laughed, and Crawt stepped closer. The red in his eyes caught the sun.

"Then let's fight." He held his arms out, and the swords appeared.

"Very well." She shifted her stance; knees bent a little, and eyes intent on him.

"Do not watch the blades. Know where I will go. Feel it."

She did. The power radiated from him into her. She knew the beat of his heart and pulse. A quiet drum in the back of her mind. She was connected to him. If it was all they had, so be it.

She marked the slight tensing of his shoulders and moved with a clear mind. She parried and blocked, ducking and spinning. He moved with unexpected grace.

Yet the thought of him coming for her and killing the soldiers was so at odds with him now. The fury and brutality of him then...

"You're distracted." He caught her, lightly pinning her with a blade. "You are an excellent sword."

"My father taught me how to hunt, and my brother taught me swordplay. We'd practise in the yard as my eldest brother read us old adventures and stories and we acted them out." Rosalin squinted and stepped away. "I always thought how romantic it would be to have my own." She laughed bitterly.

"Do you regret this? Being here."

"Never. I'd be dead by now or forced into less than pleasant circumstances."

"Being hunted to be taken into an underworld of torment are pleasant circumstances?" He tilted his head, urging her to begin again.

"I'm afraid of what will happen, but I'll never regret coming here."

He lowered his swords for a moment, and she attacked. He growled and defended.

They danced in the sun and damp air for the afternoon until weary and panting, Rosalin fell to her knees.

Crawt wasn't even out of breath. "Come." He held out his hand after retracting his swords. "I'll cook the mushrooms and grain."

She retracted her own, the sting and pain bringing tears to her eyes. She stood, with her hand in his. He turned her hand over and ran his thumb over the greyish patch where her swords appeared. She shivered at the touch and watched.

"Rosalin."

With a swallow, she looked up at the tenderness in his eyes, but Crow cawed, and Crawt whipped his head to the forest. The hairs on her arms stood up.

"There are more coming?"

"Yes."

"Let me help you."

"No. Go in, be safe."

"I can help. I'm good enough, you saw me."

"You are exceptional, but I need to keep you safe. I have done this for time beyond your understanding. I can defend us. Let me go." Crawt kissed her forehead and strode off. "Into the house," he called back as he vanished into the trees.

Fox nudged her, and she grabbed the basket and went inside. The sun began to set. She washed her face and hands, and for something to do, she cooked. This wasn't her; waiting at the window, being protected. Had she not kept herself safe for months?

And at what cost? What had she given of herself as a result? The light dimmed into full night.

Stubborn demon. Something was wrong; her stomach was uneasy and skin prickled. She opened the door, and Fox yipped and followed at her side. She went across the lawn, and heard the distant sound of fighting, running faster, she saw it some distance from the well. The ground had split, and from the fissure rose a foul stench. She skidded over the mud as quietly as possible.

A group of mangled things attacked Crawt, and he cut them down, but they climbed over him. The withered creatures attacked along with smaller demons, who were pale grey with horns. They must be as Crawt looked once.

Rosalin didn't even think, she just started fighting. Her swords bright, she slashed at two at his back. They sprang down, gurgling a cry and went for her. She thrust hard into one, pivoted and cut the head off the second.

She crouched low, cutting the leg off another, and seeking a demon; she cut off its head before it could turn to her.

All the while, Crawt took down one, only to be attacked by more that climbed up from the hole. His breath was ragged. Rosalin slashed at the small group that came for her. One cut her, and it stung, but she feinted to the side and cut it in two, while she ran through a second. She got closer to him, thinning out the group until there were nothing but corpses and no more came from the ground.

Crawt fell to his knees and retracted his swords. "What are you doing here?"

"Helping," she bit out.

He was covered in deep and oozing wounds and looked defeated.

"Let me burn them." Rosalin panted, and he only glanced at her.

"I have to close it."

Rosalin found her flint tin from inside her tunic and sparked a fire on one of the bodies. Crawt sagged down, eyes on the fissure.

In the silence, Fox ambled over to Crawt and licked his master's hand. He blinked and petted the animal before standing.

The fire took, and Rosalin dragged bodies over, making sure they all caught alight. She glanced up, stepping away from the flame and stench, and watched Crawt. Blue light surrounded him and glowed in the dark, yet it was dim. The ground trembled and the fissure closed. He sagged forward, and she went to him.

He rested his arm around her, and she held his waist. "Let's get you home."

Crawt grunted in response, and they walked back, leaving the fire to burn out.

In the kitchen, she cleaned the deep cuts on him in silence. They weren't healing. She found the salve, and he sighed as she smoothed it on the wounds. She watched them heal over.

Crawt grunted and caught up her hand from his shoulder as she rubbed it in.

"Funny, not long ago you were tending to my wounds. What's wrong?"

"The last time I made you leave it was because you were in danger, but partly because I wanted something that is not mine to have. It was a mistake to take it." Crawt closed his eyes. "Someone so beautiful, so lovely, who was not afraid..."

Rosalin swallowed, setting the pot down, she cupped his face. He pressed into it and held her hand there.

"For a moment of beauty and perfection, I have brought myself and everything else to ruin." Crawt closed his eyes.

Rosalin couldn't speak, but she held him. Falling into his lap, she buried her face into his neck and held him tight. The giant sighed, his arms slowly encircled her, and she wanted to sob.

She'd known. Hope was dangerous, and he'd given her that, but she knew what they'd done was wrong, yet it felt perfect to be in his hold. Her rightful place.

Ache

Rosalin leant back as her stomach dipped. "**W**hat do you mean by 'the last time I sent you away?'"

"This is only going to get worse." The red light in his eyes dimmed.

"Don't do this. Let me fight beside you. I've proved to you I can. I'm strong enough." She wanted to grab his horns and shake him.

He didn't speak but ran his finger down her cheek, his claw caught her skin and leaning into his touch, she waited out his thought. Sometimes he'd forget he had to speak out loud.

"All things end. All life turns to nourish the new. Nothing is forever."

"What do you mean?" Rosalin climbed off him.

"My power is spent." He frowned opening and closing his fists. "I feel it."

"Because of me?" Her breath left her body and pain curled through her.

Crawt looked up slowly and stood, holding her eye. "I want to ask something of you that I've no right to." He looked down, grimaced and shook his head. "You should go and leave this place because when I fail, the land will be overrun, and there will be no stopping what follows."

"No. Never, I will not abandon you."

He sneered. "You will."

"No."

"I will not have them take you," He roared, and she stepped away from him. "I will not let them destroy your soul and take what I gave you. They will not take who I love."

She blinked back her tears and stepped to him, reached up and clutched at his neck, he shook his head, but she held fast.

He was immovable, so she jumped and held on. His arms went around her, and she kissed him. His lips were as hot as she remembered.

He broke the kiss and stared at her. She saw the moment he gave in, and let his desire take over. Clenching his jaw, he left the kitchen still holding her and took her through the castle, gripping her tightly.

Rosalin pressed her face into his neck, dropping little kisses on tense skin, his heat and scent comforting and like home. Her heart hammered at the familiar and exciting thrill of finally being with him.

All she could do was watch, transfixed by his power as he set her down in his rooms. Grander than hers, and his huge, ornate bed dominated the room.

Crawt walked her back. He didn't speak but pulled her tunic up and off, his hands went to her trousers, pulling open the laces. All the time, his eyes never left hers.

She fell back on the bed, he lifted her legs, undressing her completely.

Her body lay open to him. He stripped, and went to her, kneeling between her legs.

"Change your mind." His voice was rougher than usual.

"Never." She reached for him, and he obliged.

He kissed her, fangs poking at her lips, he was gentle as his tongue stroked hers, and she relished it. His hesitation from the pool was gone, and she managed to keep up.

Wrapping her legs around his waist, she ran her fingers over the scars on his back, feeling every strike of a whip, every ounce of flesh taken from him, she felt aeons of pain and rage, darkness and torment, and she wept.

Crawt pulled back. "I am sorry."

She locked her arms around him. "How do you live with so much pain?"

Taking her arms from him, he held her wrists and kissed her tears. "I have for too long to count. I know nothing else."

"Not anymore, you know me." Rosalin reached up and kissed him with fierce passion. They could pretend it was true for a while.

His fangs nipped her lips, and she tasted blood. Crawt growled, pulling from her mouth, and she undulated her hips up to him. He climbed up and pushed inside her. They cried out together.

Her face didn't reach his shoulder, and he was heavy. She knew why he chose the pool for their first time. He moved, and she bit his chest. He stilled.

"My love." He cradled her head and shook.

Rosalin purred and stroked his back. "Please."

He spoke softly as he moved. "In the pool, you were sweetness that I have never known. Perfect. Beautiful."

She moaned at his words. He said everything she'd needed to hear. He whispered love to her, new and intense, and she was greedy for every word, for every movement of his hips until they grew frenzied and close. Crawt's power overwhelmed her as she held on.

When she came, the same stretched pleasure ran through her release as before. She clawed at him, demanding more, and pushed him over the edge as he took her with need. He let out a long roar, arching back. Deep in her, it was too much, and yet she needed more.

Crawt withdrew, and eased down, resting his head on the bed and caught her with his horn.

"Ow." She moved her head to the side.

"I'm sorry." He leant up, and she started laughing. "It's not funny. I could have poked a hole in you."

She laughed harder, and he raised his brow in disapproval, but she couldn't stop. Crawt sighed and lay on his back, pulling her close. She closed her eyes and listened to the thump of his heart, tracing the lines on his chest.

"Why have you resisted us?"

"You deserve better."

"Better? Than the guardian Lord who governs the magic between realms? Who else is there for me. We are one now." She kissed his chest, and he sighed, eyes fluttering closed.

"I never thought I could love. Until I saw you wander into my garden. So much anger and grief. I wanted to take it from you."

Neither managed much sleep, and when she woke from a doze to early dawn air, she was alone. She sat up, rubbing her face, sore and exhausted, but pleasantly so. She flopped back and turned over. Crawt stood naked at the window.

"What is it?"

He didn't move as she got up, and finding the air cooler, she pulled on her tunic. She stood next to him and saw what he saw. The forest, from the well outward, was dead, the black core of trees unchanged, but the barren decay spread out, almost reaching the safe paths and the garden.

He took her hand in his, turning his head. "Will you live, for me."

"How about we both do. Come with me."

He laughed but sobered and looked back to the creeping demise.

Fear closed her throat. It really was coming to an end; all would fail. She thought of the people on the caravan, the girl at the Inn, and all the innocents that had already died. "Do you think leaving you will make me happy? Because it won't. How can I live with the fact that all will come to an end? Life will fail because I didn't stand with you."

"They will win and take you. You won't die. They will rip the flesh from your body and destroy who you are."

"Together we have hope. There will be power between the two of us."

A sad smile flickered onto his face. "Get dressed."

She readied for the day, and whatever might come. In the garden, she faced the woods and felt the creep in her spine. Her arms tingled, and she knew evil was coming.

Crawt joined her a little later; he wore a newer shirt, one she'd sewn for him. The light fabric was bright in the sun, and he cupped her face.

"Ready?"

"Yes." Rosalin was afraid, deeply afraid, but she'd do anything at his side.

He murmured strange words, and his skin heated.

"What are you doing?" She squirmed, but he didn't release her. His eyes glowed, and he tilted his head back. She heard Crow caw from somewhere, and Fox pawed her leg. The world turned, and she upended, and everything vanished, and Rosalin went with it.

Magic

R osalin looked at the sky, feeling a little confused. Sitting up, she knew she wasn't home. The air tasted different and unfamiliar sounds encroached.

"Crawt?" It had been morning, and then... "The swine." She thumped the grass.

On a cliff, she, Fox and Crow sat. He'd left them there and gone back to face his end. Proud, selfish, noble, and ridiculous demon. Crow hopped down onto her leg and tilted his head to one side then the other, blinking. His tiny black eyes shone.

Fox snuffled her and licked her hand.

She stood too quickly, and the world swam. She fell back to her knees, and the view caught her breath as she gasped in the salty, frigid air.

The sea. He'd brought her to the coast. The mountain shore spanned most of the eastern coastline. Shallow beaches of dark sand edged jagged cliffs and running up the length, towns and villages on stilts in the water. A sophisticated network of communities built out from central piers.

One could travel anywhere from them. Her brothers told her stories of adventurers and monsters, and of lands across the seas. The nearest town

was nothing but a wreck, long deserted. Seabirds circled it, and beyond she saw another further on, boats enclosing it as it vanished into the distance.

She wondered if this was where here brothers fell. Rosalin let herself feel it, just for a minute before turning. Nothing but forests, hundreds of miles of trees, and no sign of the castle.

"Crawt?" She knew there'd be no answer. Pain sliced through her middle and she sat down, facing the sea. She looked at the ships. The possibility of escape at her feet.

Fox lay down beside her. He'd brought Fox and Crow to keep them safe.

"And you approve of this?" She scratched Fox's ear, and he whined. Crow squawked and flapped, hopping up and down.

"Would you go back? Would you save him?"

Fox put his head on her knee, and Crow stepped close, thrusting his head forward.

"I can't go to sea. I'll be killed before I get on a boat." She squinted out to the coastal town. Rosalin stayed there, staring out. The sun lowered behind her, and she watched the pink light fade.

Crow flew to a pack nearby that Crawt had been holding when he joined her in the garden. She opened it up. A few supplies and her spare clothes, and a small book. Standing, she shouldered it and headed down the incline and into the forest.

The steep rock and scrub gave way to dense thickets. She found no way through and skirted northwards. In the dark, the path became narrow, and her arms caught the long thorns, snagging her cloak.

Crow flapped and flew down to her from the top of the thicket, pecking at her pack.

"Fine, we'll stop." Rosalin made a small fire and ate a little fruit, huddling into her cloak, crossed legged, with Fox curled up on her lap.

She tossed down a berry for Crow, who pecked at it merrily. She remembered the book. Small and black, the thick parchment was rough and, on its pages, Crawt's scrawl.

Her skin goosed, and she ran her thumb over the words. This was what he'd been doing. He'd planned to get rid of her, knowing the end was coming. She rested her head back on the rock behind her, blinking up at the night sky.

Countless stars glittered down over her fire. Rosalin closed her eyes and remembered him underneath her. She smiled at how he made her feel, at the glow in his eyes as he arched his back in pleasure. Her throat burnt, and she sipped water from her canteen.

Leaning into the light of the fire, she read. The symbols on her body explained. Language translated. She skimmed through and went back to the beginning.

Stay safe, my love. She ran her thumb over the words, fighting tears. Anger replaced hurt. The foolish creature.

She read the meanings and power of every symbol until her eyes closed. Then she was lying in bed with Crawt looking at her.

She smiled. "What are you doing here?"

He didn't reply, but Rosalin woke, and it wasn't even dawn. Her heart ached. She packed up, and Fox ambled ahead of her as Crow flew on and circled back. He cawed and cawed until they caught up a few hours later. A substantial thicket had grown so tall, there was a small gap underneath, and she squirmed under it, wriggling through the dirt.

Brushing off her clothes, she looked around at moss-covered ancient trees, gnarled and twisted, and ferny undergrowth in dappled sunlight.

The ground trembled in a deep rumbling. Rosalin steadied herself against a trunk, and Fox curled into her legs, with his head down. Leaves fell from the trees. Small animals scurried into the thickets, and birds flew.

Crow flapped at the pack when the ground stilled as creaking in the distance cut the silence.

"What?"

He pecked at the bag. She took out the book, and he flew up. She opened it, reading again as he settled on her shoulder.

Next to an intricate symbol, one that was on her shoulder was the word: *Rise.* The power to cover distance. Huh. She must have been too tired to connect it.

Thinking of the swords, she clenched her fists, stepping back from the tree. She tilted her head back, focusing her breath, feeling the same pain, her tongue itching with the word upon it, and her mind focused on the symbol. Up. Rise.

She jumped. Her body was lighter, but she didn't go very far. Crow flew up to a high branch, and with a deep breath, she focused on where Crow landed and jumped. The ground propelled her up, she gained speed and found herself in the spot she'd envisioned.

Rosalin laughed. He'd given her so many gifts. She peered out over the rolling canopy, and she saw home in the distance, clouded in mist, almost hidden, but not from her. "I'm coming."

She jumped down, landing softly. "Now you." She opened her cloak, and Fox jumped up into her arms, she secured and tied it under him, kneeling down, and with him secured, and the book safe, she launched up.

It was weeks of travel on foot. Hopefully, it would only be a day or so using magic. Time to test her power.

She focused on a tree ahead, atop a small ridge, and focusing, she leapt high into the air and found herself on a branch, which promptly cracked under her weight, and she landed with a thump on her back.

Fox squirmed out of her hold. "That needs work." She coughed, getting her breath back. She ate some bread, oddly hungry after and yawned. It was annoying how used she'd become to sleeping in a bed again. Her body ached.

She read the book. Each symbol on her body, where it was, what it meant, and its power laid out for her. He'd given her so much of his magic and used his own. Rosalin had caused this. No, it was inevitable. The end had already begun for him.

Rosalin packed up. "Come on." She secured Fox, though he gave her a mournful look and licked her neck when she was ready.

Focusing on a valley far below, she said the word in her mind, knowing its power as she rose high into the air, moving with speed, and hopefully, accuracy.

Ruin

Fighting for breath, Rosalin fell on the damp grass by the river with a considerable distance to go before reaching the pool. Fox nudged her as she rolled over, letting him out of her cloak. "I'm fine."

He padded off and drank at the water's edge.

Sweat soaked her skin, yet she shivered. Her muscles ached, and nerves pinched. With a thick head and vision that swam, she crawled to the water, catching the red glow in her eyes as the water rippled.

She washed her face and cupping her hand, drank. Water that was once crisp tasted bitter. Leaves browned and fell in the water, vibrant greens faded, and in the still air hung an unpleasant scent.

Dull pain throbbed through her and muscles shook, but she managed to sit for a moment. Braiding her hair back, its length irking her again, she tied it off with a thread from her cloak. A little of the dried fruit revived her, and turning to Fox, he lay down, looking at her.

"What is it?"

He whined when she petted him, and the ground shook again. Crashing reverberated, echoing through the trees. Rosalin stood, wincing, but saw nothing from their lowered position.

"We need to move." Crow went ahead, and Rosalin gathered Fox up. She tied him into her cloak and with his snout on her shoulder, took flight, rising high and faster, fear and urgency driving her forward. Landing briefly, she cried out, launching up again. Every leap closed the distance.

Cold air rushed over her skin as they moved, and her mind focused on her purpose; Crawt.

The past edged into her thoughts along with Crawt's face. Finding her way to him at the end of his reign of power was a no accident. It was meant. Her focus faltered, thinking of being with him and caressing his cheek as he kissed her hand.

"I love you."

He'd smiled at her whisper and sat up, holding her close as she trembled and shook.

They descended in the air, and she couldn't stop the fall but landed slowly before stumbling onto her side.

Rosalin curled up, the pain unbearable in her limbs, and she clutched herself close. She was spent, and unwillingly, she closed her eyes. Night fell, and the cool dark soothed her as she gave in.

The sound of Crow brought her around to deep night. Stiff and sore, she eased up. "I can't. We can walk a little though." She drank and ate the last of her supplies, and they walked on, following the river. It gradually widened out until they reached the pool, where it finished and disappeared underground before reappearing at the gardens nearing dawn. The water held no current, and the pool looked stagnant.

As they climbed the hill, the stone table lay cracked and broken, and Mirelda's great oak blackened and dead. Rosalin hurried down, and the grass underfoot was dead.

Rosalin fought tears, her breathless sobs catching in her throat, and then she skidded to a halt as she emerged from the path.

A sense of inevitable end overwhelmed her at the destruction. She thought of the war, her family, and all the people she'd lost. Wiping her face, she growled and went on.

There was no sound or wind. She touched a bush, the one that had been laden with fruit and had first eaten from, but it had all rotted and fallen to the ground. The scent of decay rose up around her. Brittle leaves fell as she brushed past them.

"Crawt," she murmured, crushing a leaf into dust in her hand as she reached the gardens. The crops wilted. The vines had fallen. The fragrant plants gave nothing, and as the dawning light cast onto the palace, she saw wide cracks in the walls. The tall tower had fallen in, and debris lay strewn over the lawns.

The kitchen door was gone, and with a deep breath, she went into what was left of the kitchen. Running upstairs, the bannister disintegrated in her hold, and the treads broke underfoot. Glass smashed in from the windows covered the floor and leaves littered shards.

In his room fabric decayed and moth-eaten on his bed and curtains faded rags. The castle rumbled, and something crashed.

Fox, who'd followed, turned away, and she followed him down to the library. The history of his life had fallen to dust. She picked up a book, and it crumbled into nothing in her hands. The words lost; all the law and history of him gone. They'd taken him.

She had to go to him. There was no choice. She rested her hands over the drawers and bit her lip. Opening the map drawer, she found most of them in pieces, but the one that did not fit was intact.

Carefully unrolling it, the thick black fabric – just like her little book – showed her the way. The white well. Her skin crawled as it had before, but biting her fear back, she stepped away.

Fox lay down next to the broken chair of his master. Rosalin crouched and stroked him, but he whined.

She met his eye. "Fox, come on, we have work to do."

He didn't move, and with a shallow pant, he closed eyes.

"Fox, come on."

Nothing. Crow flew in, cawing wildly and hopped about, one wing askew, and a feather fell.

Tears burnt her eyes. "I know. I'm going to get him. I'll not return alone. I swear. Hold on."

Rosalin wasted no time and fled the crumbling palace, crossed the grounds, and without hesitation, fled into the forest. Her tears fell as she went, but she dashed them, steeling herself. Gritting her teeth as she found the dead, icy centre of the forest, mulch caught her feet. She cursed, wrenching her legs from the mud, leaving her boots, and scampered over the muck.

In the forbidden ground, she weaved in and out of the blackened and slimy trees, finding the way; drawn to it. The power pulsed through her as the trees became sparse, with the markings hot on her skin. The soft ground underfoot didn't slow her as she skipped over the filth, until she found it. The broken well that was once covered and buried, now left open and unguarded and broken in two. It was a trap. They needed her power too, but Crawt gave it to her and sent her away.

Rosalin didn't doubt his love but giving her his power served another purpose: stop their dominion. No going back now. She had to fight.

With a steady breath, she let her cloak fall and leapt high, raising her arms above her head, her swords appearing at her hands, wreathed in blue flame, and she descended into another world.

Hell

The descent took forever. Rosalin found resistance beneath her in a warm rush of air. Upending and turning, she ran her swords down the stones of the well, until it opened out into a cavern, and she landed softly on a gritty floor. She regretted not having her boots. Her swords lit the pitch-dark space, and she saw red rock all around her, sharp and jagged, and no way out that she could see.

She winced at the muffled sound of screaming that echoed in the distance.

Heading to the sounds, she found a path. Set with low stone pillars, she followed what was little more than a crude tunnel, the walls of which carved with grotesque images of torment. The stench of blood and death rose as she went in the close heat.

Hearing the shuffling of feet, she braced, squatting low. Two tall, stark white demons – like Palzine – stopped as they saw her, surprise stalling them for a moment.

In a second, they moved as one, closing the distance, lunged, and grabbed at her, but she ducked and pivoted. Searing pain shot through her arms, she gritted her teeth as one caught her wrist, and she jabbed him with her free hand.

The other moved behind her with its arm around her neck. The first demon attempted to wrestle her sword from her, but she retracted it, forcing her hand out in front and with a strangled growl, she thrust out the sword anew, straight into his chest, and rent her arm upwards, cleaving the creature in two.

The demon holding her let go, and she swung around, swords out. He ducked and stepped back. The two squared off as sweat beaded down her face and grimaced at the stench of the dead thing.

She bared her teeth, growling at the demon, feigned right, pivoted to the left, and thrust her sword into him to the hilt.

Eye to eye, she held his look, his scent tasted foul as she caught his breath, and she leant back, cutting off his head with her free arm.

Pulling her sword from his body, she let him fall and headed on. Covered in dark blood, Rosalin didn't think, she felt nothing, and became the person who lived in the forest months ago when she was a mortal.

The neglected passage opened out into a finer one. The rude carvings became detailed and rich, intricate patterns – ones like her own and Crawt's – set out in a massive mural, carved deep into the rock. The intricately laid floor and ceiling widened and heightened, and the path broke into two. She closed her eyes, seeking him, feeling for his power and her blood pulsed. She headed right, to the sound of screaming.

The corridor opened out into chambers off a broad passage, and she poked her head in one cautiously. From the ceiling hung the remains of a man with bone visible in places, and an empty eye looking at her. She watched a small mangled demon carve the flesh off the corpse. A soldier once, his uniform lay in tatters on the floor. Then the body jerked and screamed and screamed and wouldn't stop. Her eyes flickered, and she nearly stepped away. His one eye met hers as tears coursed down her face. Rosalin went cold, even for the heat of the place.

Pressing her mouth into a line, she crept into the small reeking cell, and with a single thrust killed the demon.

"Live or die?" she said, her words weak.

"Die," it rasped.

Rosalin sent him to the same fate.

The life left his face, and she turned, unable to look in any of the others. Bile sat in her throat. She hurried along as each demon went about its task in the chambers either side of her.

This had happened to Crawt. Brought here and consumed and then remade. He had done this too. Stripped of all sensibility and personhood, he'd destroyed men and made them like him.

But he'd rebelled. Rosalin pushed it back; it wasn't the time to face it.

At the end row of the cells, she met an end with no way beyond. Putting her hand on the wall, she felt it vibrate, and looking up she saw a glimmer of light outlining a door. She pushed on the stone, it nudged a little and putting all her weight behind it, the door gave. With a final shove, it opened, and she managed to squeeze through the small gap.

"Hey, what d'you do there!" The ugly voice came from down the corridor, and she slammed it shut behind her, the sounds of muffled snarls and squawking on the other side closed in.

She stood in a tiled and light chamber. Crawt hung suspended in a taut, thick chain that wrapped around him. His arms pulled up, and his feet hovered off the floor. He hung his head and didn't move with his body stretched out.

Beside him, a white stone slab lay with symbols carved into it. She looked from it to him. The demons thudded the other side of the stone door.

"Crawt," she hissed, but he didn't stir. Knowing what her fate would be, Rosalin almost smiled, looking at the creature she loved. She stretched out her arms, her swords appearing once more. If this was how she died, so be it.

Steeling herself, she stepped away from the door and turned. It shook and thudded. An arm reached through the gap as it inched open, and she cut it off, every limb that appeared, she lopped it.

When a head pushed through, she took that one off as well. She stabbed through the gap as it widened. One came through, and she sliced it in half. Demon after demon came, and she cut down each one until her arms ached, and she sobbed each breath. The door opened wide, forcing her back, and over the dead pile, a great demon walked, crushing the dead beneath his tread. Luminous white with deep red horns, black eyes, and taller than Crawt, he purred as Rosalin stumbled to the floor but scrambled to a crouch.

The thing laughed. "So, you came, just as Palzine said you would. It's a shame what you did to him. Will you cut me down too like your master attempted to before?"

"You're the first demon."

"Yes. Set with a task. Given to me as a noble purpose. One that creature rebelled against." The Master Demon raised his arm in a smooth movement, pointing his long sharp nails at Crawt. "I've waited for you for a long time. Foolish child." Long grey fangs poked out as he smiled, dropping his arm. "I'm going to rip you apart for an age. Your lover will watch as I strip every ounce of power from you and him and take back what it is mine. Ready?" The creature spoke smoothly, just like Palzine.

He lunged at her, and she dodged while he chased her like a cat with a mouse. She jumped the slab and saw a line of demons barring the door, all silvery white and smaller and weak looking, like spiders bred in the dark, and they were intent on her. She leapt high and sliced the chain that held Crawt upright, and he fell to the ground.

She landed and squared off the Lord.

With a wide grin, he bent down to her. "You cannot win."

Rosalin made no answer, her mind working quickly. She ducked low, and he lunged for her, she slid between his legs, cutting out with both swords, and he fell.

As the creature knelt up with a squealing cry, the lesser demons stepped forward. Rosalin jumped high, landing behind one, her arms jabbed and swung, lashing out in quick movements. These creatures weren't built to fight or were out of practice.

Three fell, but as she turned to finish the last, the Lord charged her and ran his horns into her back. Her breath caught her throat, and she looked down, scrabbling. She couldn't reach the wound, and his hands went around her waist, hauling her up into the air. She screamed with what felt like her last breath.

The Master Demon pulled out of her back. The wound radiated pain until she couldn't feel it. Paralysed, she watched as she was thrown down onto the table. The demon leant over her. Her vision doubled as she gasped.

Baring his teeth, he licked her blood as it fell down his face from his horn. Rosalin couldn't look away, she wanted to, but her eyes wouldn't move.

Her vision blurred and Rosalin saw Crawt holding her under the bright sun, laughing as Fox scampered across the lawns. Spring was all about them, and he kissed her hair.

She turned her face, blinking, making her eyes focus, and saw him crumpled on the floor. Keeping her gaze fixed on him, she spluttered and spoke the words as he once did. The words from the book. Heal. Heal. A chant in her mind and heart. Blood and muscle, bone and sinew working; magic rushing through her. Her flesh seared and pulled. It was a thread in her that reached to Crawt, and she pulled it. Yanking hard on the magic as the demons readied to torture her, she found strength through that pain. In an agonised breath, she lifted her hand and dabbed it in the blood that pooled around her and on the inside of her other arm, she copied the symbol as best she could with her fingers.

With a hiss, the Lord of Demons grabbed her arms, snapping them. She screamed, and the horrifying sound pierced the chamber.

The demon pulled her distorted limbs over her head, and she thrashed against it. Taking a dagger, long and glass-like, the thing raised it above her but turned sharply as a chain whipped its side.

Crawt knelt up, grunting, and swung it again. Rosalin chanted the words through her agony, arching her back off the table as she did.

Sharp, twisting pain shot through her body as her bones crunched and reset. The livid bruises faded as her skin knitted closed and she sat, watching the two demons face each other.

She stood and staggered. A dogged determination filled her, eating the pain, and she held her arms out, igniting her swords with a scream.

More demons joined them.

The Master Demon sneered and gestured to the door. "Crawt, more are coming. You will never escape, and you can never really kill me. What you've taken is not yours to keep, it must be returned from the flesh where it dwells."

The chains fell loose around Crawt's feet, he stepped out of them and ignited his own swords. As one, Crawt and Rosalin stepped forward, and in a bright angry clash, they attacked.

The others fell as they fought unarmed. Hands clawed their skin and pulled at them. Crawt took three in a sweep, as one grabbed Rosalin's leg and she fell. Turning in its grip, she lopped off the arm, and it screamed as it reared back. Cutting off its head, she turned to see Crawt fighting the Lord.

Rosalin strode up behind him and rent his arm off. Crawt took a leg. They speared him together, she sliced in one direction, and he another. After a breath, they withdrew, and Crawt staggered back as the Lord fell.

"We need to go." He barely got the words out.

Rosalin fixed her eyes on the thing on the floor. It's perfect marble skin already greying above a thick pool of blood.

"You should not have come."

"You should not have doubted me."

Retracting their swords, they looked at each other.

Crawt's eyes were dim, and he staggered. Great wounds covered his back.

"Can you make fire?"

"No, I don't have that power."

From inside her tunic, she found her flint and struck it, and sparks fell onto what was left of the demons in the cell. They went up in seconds, and Crawt and Rosalin retreated down the corridor of torment.

With a cold heart, she ended the suffering of each one. Burning what was left. The air was thick with foul smoke, and they coughed as they headed to the dark open chamber. Piercing cries rose as others discovered the fire.

"How do we get out?" She looked up, a tiny pinpoint of starlight far away was the only sign that there was a way out.

"Go up."

He took her hand, and they jumped. They fell upward, tumbling into the darkness above them. The chasm closed in, and the well narrowed until they climbed the stones upwards.

Pulling out of the broken circle, they lay in the cold filth around it, bodies steaming.

"It is not done," Crawt said in a weary whisper.

"I know." Reaching out, she took his hand.

"I do not know what will happen next."

"It doesn't matter. It's what we must do."

Crawt looked at her, the fire in his eyes returning. He smiled for a moment, resting his face on hers before murmuring, and thrust his hand into the soft ground. His voice rose, and she copied the sounds. Crawt arched his back, his words garbled, ending in a cry.

She took over, making herself sit up, keeping hold of his hand, and she reached into the soil and found his.

Their eyes met as she leant over him. She said the words with the language in her bones and power in her blood. His skin glowed blue, as did hers. The pain was electric, and she screamed.

He joined her again, and they drew strength together. The well cracked and sank down into the ground as it shook, the pull on their bodies forcing them into the mire. The trees groaned, limbs snapped off, and the ground devoured everything around them. Distant sounds of destruction closed in as they held each other, power and magic pulsed between them, and fell downwards into darkness. Every brick and stone, every ounce of power tumbled into ruin. Into them.

Rosalin screamed, clinging to Crawt as they were swallowed whole into cool dark.

Begin

☾

Crushing weight sat on Rosalin's chest, and she heard a muffled cry. Struggling, she pushed her arms up and broke free of the deep mound of earth on top of her.

Drawing a loud breath, she coughed and blinked open her eyes. She was caked in dirt, and it was pitch black all around her. The ground moved next to her, and she clawed at the soil until she found Crawt.

Brushing dirt from his face, she ran her hand along his cheek, and he took a breath, opening his eyes. Their red glow the only light in the darkness.

She laughed, tears streaked her face, leaving blue tracks.

He sat up, looking about, and growled at her.

"My love." Rosalin knelt, reaching her hand to his cheek.

He frowned, and after a moment, he cupped her chin. With a soft face, he gathered her gently and held tight. Power radiated from him, and Rosalin leant back from the intensity. He reluctantly pulled them up, still silent. For minute, they held still as understanding filtered through. It was done. They lived.

Rosalin and Crawt walked past the few remaining trees, and fog crept in. As they emerged, there was nothing left of the castle other than a scattering of rubble.

"Fox and Crow." She gasped at barren space around her that the first streaks of dawn showed them. Light crept up over the rubble, and Crawt leant his head back, soaking in the warmth.

Rosalin was dizzy, and her skin buzzed. She looked down at the brighter blue of her skin, the marks stark. His skin was vivid, and the power made the lines etching him luminous.

He tilted his head, power crackling about him. From the debris, Crow flew into the sky, and Fox scampered out. He looked younger, and his coat shone. He sat on the grass thumping his bushy tail.

Rosalin laughed.

"We're here." Crawt seemed confused.

"Yes. Like you were before."

"I thought I was dreaming."

She took his hand, and he blinked.

"What would you like?" Crawt asked evenly.

Rosalin focused, taking in what he said. "What do you mean?"

"I built the castle because I thought a great big palace was suitable for what I became." He turned to her. "This will never be over. Eventually, they will find a way. What you saw was a fraction of what is beneath. Levels of horror and evil beyond knowing. The path is gone, and the well swallowed completely. But I feel it. The link isn't severed."

"Yes." She knew it too, a forgotten undercurrent of something very wrong.

"It was the price for this power, to guard and defend the mortal realm." Sharp energy moved over his skin like lightning, but softer. He was younger, brighter, yet the same. The energy leapt to her, sharp and hot. She jumped.

Her eyes flickered at his look, turning back to the ruin as the energy dissipated. Tilting her head to the side, she shrugged and thought for a moment. "A house. A nice house. Not too big, or huge draughty rooms."

"Done."

He turned to the space before them and spread his hands, and the light crackled again. From the foundations, the ground shook rumbled, the remnants fell back into the ground, and stone shot up, twisting into walls and structure, a doorway appeared as windows formed from widening squares.

She looked at Crawt, his intense face contorted with Effort. His hands clawed and trembled.

Two floors with a large door, a tiled and sloping roof, appeared out of the rubble, and out from it, a paved yard with a step to the door.

For a minute, the patterns on his skin pulsed, and then dimmed before settling again.

As the sun rose higher, bathing the whole in bright sun, Crawt smiled, and the dead gardens sprang into life as Crawt turned to where they once stood.

"A goat?" Rosalin ventured, her voice quiet in awe. "And chickens."

"But of course." He turned back and gestured next to the house. Chickens clucked, and a goat chewed the grass.

Rosalin clapped her hands. "May I ask one other thing?"

He raised his brow.

"Mother grew roses, big red ones. She took so much pride in them."

Crawt took her hand and kissed it, and her skin tingled. Without looking from her, thorned vines grew and twisted up, leaves unfurled, and buds appeared. He led them to the house and stopping at the roses that climbed the stone, and he touched a bud with a look of wonder in his eyes. The rose bloomed, fragrant and bright. Crawt broke the stem and passed her the flower. Rosalin took it, inhaling the sweet scent and brushed the soft petals to her face.

"I've not used nearly as much power for this. Let us furnish the house." He inspected his arms and tilted his head to one side then the other, his face in a shrug before he strode in.

He looked almost impish as she followed. A solid table, comfortable chairs, a pump. A large stove.

"May I ask you a question?"

"Hmm. You will anyway." He wandered through the rooms, curtains materialising at the windows.

"How do you know what a stove looks like? Do you need to know how to make curtains to make them appear?"

He turned to her, blinked and laughed. His fangs poked out. "Always curious," he murmured, tipping her chin up.

"Yes, I really want to know."

He picked her up, and she wrapped her legs around him. His smile vanished into a frown. "Rosalin, you shouldn't have come back."

"And you should not have abandoned us. How could I have gone to sea? I'd have been hanged and set on fire. We are meant to be, don't you know? It couldn't have been an accident I came to you. I love you."

He kissed her.

"So, about the stove."

He sighed and set her down. With a dry look, he led her upstairs. A large room, with a large bed, waited for them; the thick, soft linens and covers inviting.

"Are you going to ask me about the bed too?" He leant on the wall as she picked up a slim glass vase that appeared and set the rose in it.

Rosalin started to peel off her filthy clothes with a laugh. "I do feel very rested. I wonder how long we were underground for. I could do with a bath."

Crawt slow blinked, his familiar surly demeanour returning, he led her to the bathing room. She pumped the water, naked.

He watched her with hunger. "I didn't put this one on you." He caught her arm, tracing the word she'd put on herself.

"No. I gave it myself to survive."

Silently, he picked her up and put her in the water. "Bathe. I'll join you shortly. I'm hungry."

"Good, I'm starved."

Bathed and clean, she remembered all that she saw. Her hands shook, sadness filling her heart. The suffering of Crawt, of those men, of herself, sat heavy in her mind. She feared it always would, but they had time together now. Time to recover.

Crawt returned – clean himself – and helped her out of the bath. He dried her off and carried her to bed.

"I missed you."

Her face crumpled, and they held each other close. "What happened?"

"Stop asking so many questions." Crawt tried to kiss her, and she pulled away. Sighing in defeat, he rested back. "There were so many. I couldn't stop them. They bound my arms, and the chains were so strong, I couldn't fight. There were dozens, and I was swarmed."

They ate.

"I'd never live with myself if I left you to that fate, and the world."

He took her plate, and kissed her, falling into a rhythm, his tongue reassuring her, and hands caressing her body.

He entered with need, and she met him. Furious, and desperate, a keen reunion of love. But as they moved as one, she felt power like no other. Her skin prickled with it, their markings glowing. He called her name as he turned them over, eyes devouring her movements as she grew bold over him.

"You're so beautiful," he reached up, hand on her heart. "I thought of you when they came for me and I pictured you with me. In my arms. Comforting me. You gave me strength. Now we're here. Together."

"Always."

Sitting up, he kissed her.

A beginning, a start, one of hope and love. Full of questions and challenges to come, but as long as it was the two of them, Rosalin didn't care. He was hers.

New World

Fox yipped. His tail wagged, and he leapt over the grass, finding it warm under his paws. Master and Rosalin laughed in the yard, and he sat, watching them with the chickens. Fox licked his lips, knowing he'd get an egg later.

He trotted into the newly green forest, his energy burnt as it had once many moons and lives past, and his companion of all that time, cawed and flew ahead.

They scampered to the edges of their magical realm, over brook and hill, through woods and rocks until reaching the great thickets. The border that no mortal crossed, except for Rosalin. Along the deep, narrow crevasse, they found their way to the coast, scampering over the mossy mountains until they reached the sea.

Fox snuffled the ground and air and cocked his head as sea birds circled and glided, kiting the sharp breeze.

The sea was a mystery to him, what wonders lay beyond?

Crow landed beside him. **Why are we here, old friend?**

Did you think we'd succeed? Fox turned from the soothing water.

No, I thought our time had come, as all things turn and end. Crow hopped a little, his beady eyes assessing his friend.

And begin again. Fox squinted his eyes at the scents on the wind.

They do. Wily creature, did you know?

I knew. You see what is from above, and I see from afar.

You were intent on her from the moment you spotted her. I did wonder. I thought it was the novelty of another. How did you know?

Fox lay, watching a boat set sail. *We've watched his power fail for a kingdom of men. This world has changed, and it will not be his power that fails in the end, it will be that men take the wood. We will fade into nothing and be hidden. It has already begun. But you have seen this.*

Yes. From the south.

Fox turned from the sea, knowing he'd never see it again, and the pair headed south, to the desolate war wastes. Monuments to the dead rose from the ground, and heaped graves were still fresh enough to bring carrion. No seed or life dwelt in the war wastes.

They passed through the world of mortals. Of lies and finite need, and hidden magic. Rounding north, they came to it. Trees cut down and houses in their place. For people knew no danger other than by their own hands.

What will become of us? Crow cawed and flapped.

We will endure. For the guardian must endure while the realm exists. The world will fall once more. He licked the scent of the air.

You've spent too long with him and speak only in riddle.

Fox wrapped his bushy tail around his feet. *The smell of mortals is very strong and sour. She never smelt like that. She was meant.*

Crow flew up into a tree and squawked loudly.

Fox spied a small rabbit and took off in hunt but lost it in a bush.

For all your wisdom, you're a poor hunter.

Fox licked his lips and scampered away. They returned home, and it was dark. A full pink moon lit the way and for the first time in many years, the evil that encroached was absent.

Crawt was in the new and smaller kitchen. He offered seed and fruit to Crow and offered the same but with an egg and a saucer of milk for Fox.

"There you are." He patted Fox with a soft smile.

Fox lapped the milk.

Crow flew in above him and perched on the back of a chair and Fox yawned, curling up by the still warm stove. His paws were cold, and he tucked them underneath his belly and tail.

"Don't tell me then." Crawt grumbled and moved off.

Crow and Fox looked at each other.

At least he's not alone now. Crow huddled in on himself.

Yes, and they will be content, even faded from the world. I am happy for it. Fox yawned and closed his eyes.

What do you mean, the world will fall once more?

Fox peeled open one eye and closed it again. *Magic is not limited to this place. There are other things hidden beyond even my sight. Things that are dark and tangled and dwell across the sea. It will come to us. One day. But not for many years. I think.* He lifted his head. *It is not an exact art. Just as when you look beyond you see all but not at once.*

I see much. None of it welcome.

It never is with you. Go to sleep. We've died and been resurrected, I need some rest, old friend.

Crow squawked and ruffled before closing his beady eyes.

Fox laughed to himself and went back to sleep. He wouldn't dream of the darkness again, or the death that took him. Or the pain of coming back.

The guardian was restored, as was he, and for now, it was enough.

The End

40847369R00073

Printed in Poland
by Amazon Fulfillment
Poland Sp. z o.o., Wrocław

25159019R00068

Printed in Poland
by Amazon Fulfillment
Poland Sp. z o.o., Wrocław